George Abiah Hibbard

Nowadays and Other Stories

George Abiah Hibbard

Nowadays and Other Stories

ISBN/EAN: 9783744747387

Printed in Europe, USA, Canada, Australia, Japan

Cover: Foto ©Andreas Hilbeck / pixelio.de

More available books at **www.hansebooks.com**

NOWADAYS
AND
OTHER STORIES

GEORGE A. HIBBARD

'3 hf t.

BER!? .D SMIT+

14C Pacific ·

"STANDING HAND IN HAND."

[See Page 49.]

NOWADAYS

AND OTHER STORIES

By GEORGE A. HIBBARD

AUTHOR OF

"IDUNA, AND OTHER STORIES" ETC., ETC.

ILLUSTRATED

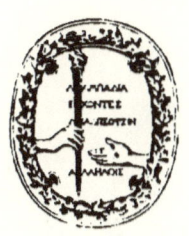

NEW YORK

HARPER & BROTHERS PUBLISHERS

1893

CONTENTS

	PAGE
NOWADAYS	I
"THERE'S NOTHING HALF SO SWEET IN LIFE"	37
"A MAD WORLD, MY MASTERS"	63
"GUILTY SIR GUY"	105
IN THE MIDST OF LIFE	153
A FLIRT	193

ILLUSTRATIONS

"STANDING HAND IN HAND" . . . *Frontispiece.*

" EDITH HAD DRAWN THE CURTAIN
     ABOUT HER " . . . . *Facing p.* 72

" THE ROOM HAD BECOME QUITE
     DARK " . . . . " 198

" BOTH WERE SILENT FOR A MO-
     MENT " . . . . " 266

NOWADAYS

Nowadays.

As Philip Santvoord steps out of the door-way he glances at the old butler, who, after giving him his hat and stick, stands with one hand on the outer door-knob, in an attitude of perfect deference, yet without losing that severe look which shows that such as he grow old with increasing doubt and live mainly to state objections. He had been in the house in the time of Philip's father. He was as much an inheritance as the "Juno" Madeira, and as incrusted with fine old habitudes as the bottles of that incomparable wine with incremental dust, and in such an old family servant certain inward reservations semi-openly expressed, as to the doings of Philip's generation in general and Philip's doings in particular, were only natural and to be expected.

"The flowers will be sent as I directed?"

"Yes, Mr Philip."

"And Wilson is to be here with the cart at half-past five—not five, mind."

"Yes, Mr. Philip."

A great deal might happen, as Santvoord knew, before afternoon, a great deal of vital importance to him, but that was no reason why any one — nowadays — should bother himself by disarranging the programme of his day.

Philip paused for a moment and then added, "That will be all."

The old butler, disapprobation in every line of his face, turned and shut the door with a moderate bang, which sounded like a well-bred ban upon all modern devices.

As Philip walked with quick but unhurried tread along the cross-street his lips just moved, and he hummed to himself the latest plaintive melody that had been wafted across the world from some London music hall. A score of things awaited his attention downtown; he had every reason to walk with a heavy heart and bent brow; but still he hummed and whistled the simple

air, as pretty and as common as the little
singer who had first given it success at
"The Empire" or "The Alhambra," with
the aspect of a man who had not a care in
the world. Is it not to-day—nowadays—
when no obtruding thought should distract,
no intruding memory weaken; when the
present is the focus of so much that there
is no time for regret or apprehension? And
so Santvoord walked briskly along the narrow side-street, filled with the animation of
the late-stirring city life, cheerfully, almost
gayly, ready to meet what the day had in
store for him — like the school-master of
Lynn when he confronted the jury that was
to give him life or death, "equal to either
fortune."

It might certainly be thought a trifle agi-
tating to begin the day with the consciousness that before nightfall one may be either
a pauper or a millionnaire, with the chances
largely in favor of the former. And this
was the predicament in which Santvoord
found himself; this the prospect he was
compelled to face on this particular morning. Yet it all seemed to him in the regular

order of things, for none more thoroughly than he lived the life of his time, when all is possible and anything probable—if it be only sufficiently strange and sudden—and when such change as might come to him he felt would be strictly "all in the day's work" of the day—of to day.

For the day was a part of these strange days in which we live, and the exact moment in which he was living and breathing and having his being was a small fraction of that most marvellous of all time—the time that we know as nowadays.

Nowadays.

Nowadays, when the world spins so very rapidly down the "grooves of time" that a strange vertigo makes us light-headed; nowadays, when the beliefs, the hopes, the fears that have brought us so far are cast by the roadside as *impedimenta* in the on-rush; nowadays, when we have "changed all that," and change is but the beginning of change. Nowadays, when the clash of battle is the loudest, the contest the fiercest, the weapons of longest range and keenest edge; when gunpowder seems slow and dynamite

almost ineffective, when heroism abides although chivalry is gone, when sacrifice ex-
ists although policy controls. Nowadays,
when the pace is so great that to stumble
is to be overrun, but when failure yesterday
may be success to-day or at latest to-morrow. Nowadays, which is like all other
days and yet so unlike any. Nowadays,
when every day works wonders the sight
of which would have made Prospero break
his staff and "drown" his book deeper
"than did ever plummet sound."

Nowadays.

Nowadays, when nothing is so distant
that it may not touch you; nothing, however
close, so near that you can wholly understand its consequences. Nowadays, when
the difficulties of a South American republic
can convulse European money centres, can
embarrass the American financial world, and
can on this morning send Philip Santvoord,
an American citizen, resident in this city of
New York, running up the stairs leading to
that iron châlet on stilts known as the ——
Street station of the Sixth Avenue "elevated" at quicker pace than he would have

used if there had been no such trouble; for so remote, so near, so quick are causes, so widespread, so ramified their consequences —nowadays.

If in nothing else, Santvoord differed from most of his contemporaries in this— he thought very little about himself; he hardly ever had time. He had always lived too thoroughly the complex life of nowadays—was too much a part of the time — to recognize how characteristic he really was; for to be so completely absorbed in a thing, so assimilated with all around, is to lose self-consciousness, to become insensible, as it were, of one's own identity. Therefore he did not recognize anything exceptional in his position this morning, considering it, if he gave it exact thought at all, only something uncomfortable, something slightly disturbing, yet natural and quite as it ought to be. How could it, all things considered, possibly be otherwise when, with all else, the desires, demands, needs of nowadays beset and possess men as did the devils of old, inexorable imps that no exorcism can cast out?

Had not his inheritance—the fortune old Santvoord had derived from his lazy-going China trade, and which had once looked so magnificent — become, in comparison with the wealth of nowadays, something really inconsiderable ? And would he not be recreant to the faith and duty of his order if he did not take the field and seek to win as others all about him were doing ?

Rushing along in mid-air, the crowded glittering street below, the empty, glowing sky above, with stretches of unequal roofs on either side leading the eye to a horizon jagged with towers and chimneys, or now shut in between walls that blocked the view, it seemed to Santvoord, as it has seemed to others even less imaginative, that he was being lightly borne through space, in a magical realization in practical nowadays of the flying carpet of Scheherezade's tale. Glancing about the car, he nodded to three or four men whom he knew, noticing, as he did this, more than one wrinkled brow and thoughtful, absent look. A panic was imminent. Before the gas had blazed or the electric lights had

shone the evening previous, the news of
the turn in affairs had been flashed uptown. It had been an anxious day, the
market had been unsteady, and there had
been a shiver of apprehension. At night,
hotel corridors had been crowded with
curious or excited men ; wise " I-told-you-
so's," were frequent in all the clubs. This
morning the excitement had the quiet of
intensity, and men were hastening " downtown " with the aspect of reserves hurried
on to a doubtful battle-field.

The evident but suppressed agitation of
those about him was assuring to Santvoord.
He felt as the duellist might when he sees
his adversary tremble as he comes on the
ground. These whom he knew in the car,
or such as these, were to be his adversaries ;
and to one of his instincts, his training, his
time—to one living nowadays—to whom
the philosophy of him of Malmesbury, that
life is warfare, seems practically true—any
sign of weakness in humanity, which to him
existed only to be overcome, gave a certain
stringent pleasure. He himself felt no fear,
no point of alarm touched him, no shade of

apprehension stole over any faculty; there
was a strain of exhilaration rather—exhilaration such as is sometimes given by the
spur of keen pain. He might have to give
up everything, even the city he loved so well
— the city that held no secrets from him,
that he knew with knowledge so inwrought
in his nature as to seem almost instinct;
the knowledge the Indian has of the prairie,
the Arab of the desert; the knowledge that
only the long-dweller in a city can obtain of
the peopled wilderness it in one sense is.
He might have to give up the costly appli-
ances of this incongruous modern life—
that life in which the vestiges of yesterday
and the aspects of to-day are so strangely
mingled in one mass of anomalousness; he
might be compelled to yield up all consid·
erable place in the harlequin existence of
nowadays, when the world, counting by its
centuries, will soon pass from its " teens,"
and, with the exultant joy of a young prod-
igal, at last come into full possession of
its own, stand ready for a " good time,"
but still rather appalled by the thought of
grave responsibilities and great possibilities.

" Bleecker !" called the conductor.

The shout startled him. He must soon leave the train.

And Madeleine? With all the force with which a thought that we have striven to disregard and keep down finally asserts itself, with all the confused arrearage of doubt, dismay, and conjecture with which such a thought at last arises, the idea of Madeleine Verschoyle suddenly arose in his mind, and filled it to the exclusion of all else. He thought of her as he had seen her at the opera the night before. The party with which she came had entered late, and as she slowly advanced to the front of the box before unoccupied — the only break and vacancy in the whole glittering tier—he, turning with many another, saw her, and for the thousandth time thought how noticeable if not beautiful she was ; for there was nothing accustomed in her aspect ; only a beholder with all modern perceptions, informed by all modern acquirement, could really realize her loveliness. To the *un-illuminati* of the time her face was illegible, her grace mere

motion. She was often thought "plain"
by those who "seeing, could not see."
The subtle charm, the quick look of sudden and complete apprehension, the manner woven in finest tissue, its warp of
natural tendencies, its woof spun from the
world's best experiences—these in her were
as nothing to most, but Santvoord had recognized her at once for what she was, an
heiress "of all the ages," and in full possession of her freehold. She was as thoroughly a creature of the day as he was
himself, and he knew it. She announced
that she was modern, and she rejoiced
in it.

When Santvoord for the first time met
her and took her in to dinner, she had allowed him to ask questions, while she only
gave answers—the safer opening, a sort of
queen's gambit in the game, all things considered; but as she rose she turned swiftly
upon him, and without prelude or provoca-
tion said, simply,

"I wish you would come and see me."

And now they were engaged.

It had been "announced" for some time,

and had received society's fullest approval ;
for was he not one whose position was un-
exceptionable and whose prospects were
excellent ?

Loss, failure, ruin, might very well mean
the annulment of their betrothal ; for Santvoord, if he indulged in illusions about
anything, certainly entertained none about
himself. He had never looked upon the
engagement in any other than a very practical way. He never thought that Madeleine
cared for him with any of the absorbing, unreasoning fervor of the lovelorn maiden of
unmitigated romance. She had too many interests in her busy life to make that possible.
She was no simple Marguerite, who might
make answer that she had "time enough"
to think of him ; indeed, he doubted if she
lost any time in such weak and unbecoming
way. She was a very modern young person,
living in a time when everything has suffered extension but the twenty-four hours,
when there is twice as much of everything
except the time in which everything must
be done, and she could hardly be expected
to waste in sentiment what should be em-

ployed upon society. So Santvoord had
thought in the enforced rapidity even of
thought nowadays, but he really had no
more attempted to comprehend the exact
state of her feeling as to him than he had
to analyze his for her. Facts are the things
—nowadays—and it was a fact that they
were engaged. Would any reasonable person think of going beyond that—of dragging
in wholly unnecessary considerations in the
way of feelings and fancies when there was
the undisputed fact itself? Certainly not—
nowadays. Why was she really marrying
him? In the rare and brief interviews their
busy lives permitted they had talked but little of what might be called sentimentality.
There was so much of substance in their
daily existence, so much of actual and vivid
interest ready at hand for their discussion,
that they had usually parted in a hurried,
surprised fashion, allowing little time for any
expression of emotional superfluities. It almost seemed as if they were astonished to
find themselves in any such position, and as
if it made them, what neither had ever been
before, a little shy and awkward.

As he looked back upon it now, it seemed
to him that there had been, after all, an un-
satisfying poverty in their relations, a "thin-
ness," a lack of "tone," something wanting.
He glanced out of the window impatiently,
as one looks quickly around when thought
annoys.   How the signs of the shops and
offices were crowded on the walls! He felt
that it would have been better if he, if she,
had not taken everything so much as a matter of course. And then he stared along the
car. But could it have been helped? What
else would have been possible—nowadays?
In a week or less it all probably would be
ended, and so what did it matter? She had
undoubtedly said "yes" so promptly when
he had so abruptly asked the question over
which so many coyly, doubtfully hesitate,
for the reason that he was so plainly "suitable"; but now should his suitableness be
ended there would be no reason why the affair should go on.   Strange that what had
been hitherto satisfactory should suddenly
appear so incomplete!   Perhaps she had
only consented to marry him because her
father had wished her to do so, for that such

was the paternal desire had been very clear
to Santvoord from the first. Old Verschoyle,
as every one knew, was "temporarily embarrassed." But there had never been a
time within the memory of the oldest diner-
out when Verschoyle had not been "temporarily embarrassed"—in such embarrassment, however, as did not interfere with his
consumption of viand or vintage, with his
country house or his city house, his mem-
bership of the best clubs, or even the main-
tenance of a very creditable racing - stable.
His was one of those remarkable existences
in which ways and means seem wholly in-
commensurate with conditions and results,
one of those who nowadays appear to possess some substitute for that old horn of
plenty which its owner could fill at will with
whatever he desired. But everybody knew
that with Verschoyle's death there would
come an end of all these good things.
And none understood better than the old
man himself how fearfully near that formi-
dable end always was. What was to become
of Madeleine? She had various aunts, estimable maiden ladies, living in a small

2

Georgian town, but would it be possible
for this radiant creature to lead other than
the modish life to which she had always
been accustomed ? Verschoyle would certainly have thought it no more possible for
her to so change existence than for himself ;
and what, concluded Santvoord, as the train
swung around a sharp corner and almost
seemed to graze the crumbling edge of the
blackened building, could be more natural
than the arrangement of the match by this
highly presentable sinner, this upper-world-
ling of threescore — of the marriage of his
only child to his " dear young friend Santvoord," who could now and then so easily
let him into a " good thing," and whose
methods were so thoroughly the masculine
complement of his daughter's modes ? And
so, he thought, his fortune and his lady-love
might be taken from him together. Some
Sir Marmaduke, riding away on a " milk-
white steed," and bidding farewell at once
to his ancestral acres and a somewhat lach-
rymose Lady Alice, might excite interest if
not respect ; but Philip Santvoord hurrying
downtown on the " elevated," uncertain

whether he may not lose a fortune sufficient to have reinstated any Sir Marmaduke and have bought out the adjoining estate of Lady Alice's noble father, doubtful whether Madeleine Verschoyle would be constant to him, is really a very matter - of - fact figure. But such is the unfairness of fate, such the lot of those who live nowadays, when even romance, as Halleck sings, is not what it was.

"Gone are the plumes and pennons gay
Of young Romance;
There linger but her ruins gray,
And broken lance.

"'Tis a new world—no more to maid,
Warrior, or bard is homage paid;
The bay-tree's, laurel's, myrtle's shade
Men's thoughts resign ;
Heaven placed us here to vote and trade,
Twin tasks divine '"

" Rector !" shouted the conductor.

As Santvoord hurried up Broadway to the " Street "—so great that, like the king of France, it requires no title—the drays, the carts, the lighter business wagons, the stages, rumbled, rattled, toiled, or dashed over the pavement as usual ; the crowd on

the sidewalk was no denser, no more hurried, than on other mornings. Broadway,
that avenue that leads to a continent, was
unchanged and, as always, ugly, bristling,
inspiriting. But the scant street itself —
highway to success, thoroughfare to failure
—wore an uncommon aspect. Messenger-
boys run in and out, through agitated hundreds; clerks with anxious, almost frightened look hasten up and down and across
the narrow way; the continuous clatter of
telegraph instruments, as the rattle of in-
fantry fire in the contest after the skirmish-
line has been driven in, can almost be heard
on the sidewalk. Men can hardly avoid col-
lision in their haste. Some meet, stop, and,
while speaking with one another, are pushed
apart by hurrying numbers, or are driven
to the gutter, where a broken sentence is
finished, or perhaps, in subdued whispers,
some eager question put. The great desire is for information; knowledge of anything, everything, that can in the remotest
way indicate how things are going; even
the drifting straws of gossip that can show
how the wind — that may be a squall, that

may be a tornado—is blowing are eagerly
caught up, and minute by minute from all
over the world pour in "cables" giving
orders, asking questions, bearing advice,
admonition, injunction ; offering support,
withdrawing aid ; carrying hope, creating
despair. News from Threadneedle Street,
reports from the Bourse, the funds falling,
rentes going down. There is excitement the
world over ; in dark Hamburg counting-
rooms, in hot Calcutta banks, the effects
of the financial shock have been felt, and
everywhere the outcome of this day is awaited anxiously, for nowadays the peoples of
the earth are bound together by golden ties,
and what ambition, faith, fanaticism, or the
theories of men have failed to accomplish,
the need or greed of gain has done, and the
world is now really united in the great Fed-
eration of Trade. With the opening of the
Exchange more would be known ; the test
of actual transaction might prove much.
As the time approaches, the steps of the
building are crowded, the street in front
almost blocked. Along the sidewalk, up
and down, are looser clusters and groups

of excited men. It is a strange gathering.
Only nowadays can its like be seen; so
many so moved by such really sordid motives, uninfluenced for one instant by the
slightest consideration of the general weal
or woe ; a struggling, agitated mass, each
stirred only by his own self-interest; a
throng without the significance evident and
felt when thousands pulsate to the beat of
some single thought, some dominant idea,
when assemblages of men have the impressiveness of Niagara. It is little if anything
more than a well-dressed rabble. But what
matter ? A crusade never created anything,
it only destroyed. Philanthropy never built
a city or a railroad. It is "business" that
does the business, and "business" is the
business nowadays.

Perplexing, bewildering nowadays !

As Santvoord sits at his table in his
rooms in the Universal Trust Building the
noises from without can only be heard as a
distant murmur. While he tears open de-
spatches and glances at letters, he loses for
the moment acute consciousness of what at
least is a crisis important to him.

And now the hour of opening had come
and passed. Every one is selling, selling,
madly, wildly, and prices are going down.
If this continues all is lost, and panic, and
all that panic entails, must follow. Men set
their teeth and wait, uncertain what the next
minute may bring; while all of them pray
for the hour when strife must cease, and
there may be chance to count the loss or
gain. A point is touched below any the
most imbittered "bear" had imagined possible, and consternation drives all in rout
before it. Margins that were thought more
than ample have been swallowed up, and a
second line of defence has in many cases
been lost. Philip feels that all is over.
The last call has strained every resource,
and the next will find him helpless. There
is nothing further he can do. Matters have
passed beyond his control; only a sudden
rise can save him. He feels that it would
be a relief to lock the door, let the storm
rage, and not receive news of its progress
until all was over and decided.

In a large breakfast-room in an uptown

house a young girl sat facing an old man.
Although different in age, in the face of each
was the same expression of indefinite dissat-
isfaction, of very definite restlessness—the
lines with which the present makes its sign-
manual upon its own.

The old man threw down the paper at
which he had just glanced; it fell upon
others that he had already cast aside.

"It looks ominous," he said; "but it
may be only a scare, a flurry, after all."

"Why should we distress ourselves?"
asked the girl, carelessly. "What have we
to do with the stock-market?"

"No one," answered Verschoyle, "is so
high or so low that he can affect to disregard what happens there—not nowadays."

"Nowadays!" half exclaimed Madeleine,
contemptuously. "Your fetich."

"Yes, nowadays," interrupted Verschoyle;
"and no one worships the fetich more de-
voutly than yourself. Don't you boast that
you live only in the present, with the present, and for the present?"

"I don't think I ever made it a boast,"
said the girl, quietly.

"But you have said it," he replied, rather petulantly; "and it is a good thing that you have felt it. If you had been other than you are, I would not have felt so secure about you. You know my position."

"We have always been in a ' position,' " said the girl. "I suppose we shall find enough to eat. Pretty much every one does."

"Eat!" exclaimed Verschoyle, impatiently. "Eat! There are appetites sharper than hunger nowadays ; needs, necessaries of life, more to such as you and I than food and drink. Eat! As if luxuries were not your necessities! You—one of the most artificial creatures that ever existed — a young woman of to-day!"

"I wonder if I am?" said the girl.

"You? You'd die from want if you couldn't have what wealth gives. That is the reason why I was in favor of this engagement with young Santvoord. It had to be. *Noblesse oblige.* A weak motto. We've a better, truer, stronger: The times compel. I've always lived up to it and lived by it, and so have you and Santvoord. Everybody said he was rich ; not so rich as some, but rich enough to keep you from what would be destitution to you. I thought it was for the best, but now—"

" Now ?" said Madeleine, quickly looking up. " What do you mean?"

" Mean ?" said the old man, fretfully. " I mean that he would not let well enough alone, that, like all the rest of us, he has been trying it on in stocks, and is likely to be hard hit, even if he does not lose all he has. I heard all about it at the club last night, and if there is a panic to day—"

The girl did not notice that her father had not finished the sentence. She sat gazing intently, vacantly, out of the window.

" What do you say to that ?" asked Verschoyle.

" Is there anything for me to say ?"

" You cannot marry a poor man."

Madeleine did not speak.

" It is impossible for such as you—nowadays," said the father.

" What do you know about me ?" demanded the daughter, quickly.

" Enough to know that," he answered, in slight astonishment. " What do you mean ?"

"I mean," said the girl, "I have learned a great deal in the last few weeks. You have been too much occupied to know much about me. We are all too much occupied to know much about each other."

"Slightly heroic in manner," he remonstrated, "and altogether out of place."

"Nowadays," she added, rather scornfully. "But I am not heroic or melodramatic."

"You are very strange this morning."

"I am not. I am myself. I can easily understand that I may seem strange to you. Absolutely you know nothing about me. You cannot say what I would or what I would not do."

"Would you marry Philip Santvoord without a penny?"

She did not answer.

"If you would," he said, "I would not consent to it. I know too well the trouble, the misery that would follow."

She was still silent.

"You," he continued—"none of us, can change a nature. You have the hunger of to-day for all that to-day can give, and

without wealth that hunger cannot be ap-
peased."

"Philip," she suddenly asked, "is in
trouble?"

"Unquestionably."

"He has not told me that he feared
trouble."

"Would such a one as he be apt to do so
—nowadays?" sneered the old man.

The girl arose as if to leave the room.

"You are going out?" asked the father.

"Yes."

"True, I had forgotten. You must see
Mrs. Thirleston to-day. Her dinners begin
in a fortnight. As you have said, it is important that you should be at the first; especially if His Royal Highness is there, as
he surely will be if he comes to this country.
Give her my profoundest regards if you see
her."

"I will," said Madeleine, "if I see her."

"I was to give this to you, and to no one
else," said a servant evidently belonging to
a "smart" establishment, as he held out a
note to Santvoord.

With the first touch of nervousness that
he had shown, Santvoord tore open the en-
velope and read the few hurried words written upon the enclosed card almost at a
glance.

" I am in the brougham in the street. If it is possible for you to get away follow William, who will
bring you where I am. I want to see you as soon
as I can, please. M."

Madeleine wished to see him, and at
once. Why not do as she asked? Perhaps it would be better that he should, let
what would come. He could accomplish
little by remaining ; things had passed beyond his control.

Again in the street. The tumult is una·
bated ; it is even intensified. Where such
interests contend, where such a tremendous
game is being played, no man, not even a
mere spectator, can stand near and not
catch something of the excitement of the
hour. The sidewalks are more crowded
than before. Human beings, too absorbed
to feel their existence, flow in currents and

counter-currents, or eddy around some central point where some one of their kind proclaims something—anything.

Money and time. Here a group with faces set in rigid lines stands silent, expectant, uncertain what the next minute may bring. Time and money! A moment, an hour, hundreds or thousands or millions, as may befit the particular needs.

Santvoord and the footman, with many a sturdy push, struggle through the throng and gain the quiet of the upper part of the street. But the man does not stop here. Pausing for a moment on the curbstone at Broadway, he awaits a chance to make his way through the flood of vehicles that struggle and crush along the pavement, and then, followed closely by Santvoord, hurries quickly across.

In front of the great, grim church that stands with fixed gaze looking down Wall Street, threatening and admonitory — in front of that church that stands as Savonarola might have stood, pausing before declamation against the luxury and greed of an older capital, Santvoord saw drawn up to the sidewalk an accurately equipped brougham which he recognized as the Verschoyle carriage.

Just beyond the high iron fence, within the church-yard, was Madeleine herself. Without speaking, he walked with her down one of the gravel-paths that run among the sallow grave-stones.

"Do you think that what I have done is strange?" she asked, when the din of the street was slightly diminished by the distance.

"Yes—no," answered Santvoord, hesitatingly.

"I think it is," said Madeleine. "It certainly is the last thing in the world that I should have thought I would do."

Philip did not speak.

"I heard that you were in trouble," she continued, "and I came."

He glanced at her in quick surprise.

"I knew that you would be surprised," she went on; "I am surprised myself. It is not what I should think any one of us would do—nowadays."

Nowadays.

He knew that in the great room of the not-distant building men were already shouting in contest, in conflict strenuous almost as actual warfare. He knew that on that field men animated only by the one passion for gain, with firm, set mouths and rigid brows, were struggling in such absorbing intensity of strife that consciousness of time, space, life, of everything but gain, gain, was lost. And all this hardly more than a block away, while here, as a child's fingers might part and play with the gray hair of age, the wind shook and dallied with the sere grasses of autumn growing limply around the gravestones, and the mild sunlight fell through the thinning leaves of the trees as if in smiling benediction upon those who knew no contention in their rest. No graveyard upon a country hill-side was more peaceful.

Confused, conflicting nowadays.

"I wanted to tell you that I was sorry," continued Madeleine. "We have never, I think, known each other very well, and I thought that you might not know"—and she, the girl whom hitherto no embarrassment could discomfit, no surprise startle, hesitated—"that I was sorry."

"Thank you," said Philip, simply. "Then you really care?"

"Why, do you not know—now?" and she looked quickly up.

"I did not know. How could I?" he answered. "I will know now. I could not bear to doubt it. And, Madeleine—"

"I think," she interrupted, "that I have wanted to tell you a long time that I cared;" and as she turned quickly away she did not see the light of gladness that shone in his eyes.

"And," he said, "even if everything else went, there would still be—"

"Everything, I hope," she interrupted again, and she held out her hand, which he seized and held in both his.

"Madeleine," he almost whispered.

"I think," she said—it was a strange waywardness, for she would not let him speak now—"that we have been living in some strange mistake. We all do nowadays. And we—like every one else—we have taken too much for granted. We allowed other

3

thoughts, other interests — miserable little transient things—to drive out the great real ones. We acted "—and she laughed gayly —" as if we were afraid that 'caring' would be a bore to us. We shirked what was serious as if it were going to be troublesome, as we all do nowadays. It needed something big to show us ourselves — our real true selves."

They had just made the circuit of the graveyard, and now stood before the church door, the massive tower rising high above them.

" But, Madeleine—"

" Let us go in," she said, quickly.

There was hardly any one in the church. The roar of the outside world came to them now as only a deep, soothing murmur. Santvoord at first hardly realized where he was. Then the softened light, the gentle stillness, the hallowed influences of the place, the only half-felt consciousness of the amazing rapture which was so deep that it even now had a touch of fear—all these humbled him into wondering thankfulness, thrilled him with strange elation.

She let him take her hand again as they sat side by side in the nearest pew.

"We will make no more mistakes," he said.

"No," she said, and sank to her knees and hid her face in her hands.

And all this is possible, for is it not—nowadays?

Nowadays.

"THERE'S NOTHING HALF SO SWEET IN LIFE"

"THERE'S NOTHING HALF SO SWEET IN LIFE"

The building could hardly be said to be specialized by anything except excessive newness, although it might be readily described generically as one of the very finest specimens of the severest type of Neo-American municipal architecture on the continent. The most malignant political opponent of the party in power shrank abashed by its austerity, angularity, and general air of being for what it was intended and for nothing else, from proffering any charge of jobbery. It stood in and of itself an apparently perfect refutation of any such suspicion. All over it told of retrenchment and reform—in its trim, clean brick-work; in its scant stone trimmings, placed, it would seem, rather for the purpose of reminding the beholder that

costly and useless ornament had been rigorously excluded than for any adorning quality of their own; in every fold of the great
zinc cornice, rising high above the actual
roof and protruding far over the street —
everywhere it bore indications that the most
direct attainment of the end in view had
been sought, not at any price by any means,
but rather at the smallest price for which
any one had been found willing to contract.

The weather, too, might have seemed to
the wildly imaginative something contracted
for by the city's government — something,
however, that had not been so successful a
bargain as the building—for it was a miser-
ably poor affair, a mere "scamped job." It
ran through all the changes from rain to
hail and sleet to snow and back again; it
melted; it froze; it exhausted its whole
repertory, and through all variations the
wind now whistled, now howled, a dismal
accompaniment. St. Patrick — a pleasant
immortality to him — must, in addition to
his other estimable qualities, have been a
saint of singular unselfishness and self-ab-
negation, for certainly only a being without

a particle of the self-seeking spirit would
have consented to take the 17th of March
—generally about the most unpleasant day
in the year—for his own. With true Irish
carelessness he must have accepted what
none other in the calendar could be brought
to consider. It was a perfect St. Patrick's
day—in the evening, and the landscape—
the moon, having risen as the hours advanced, shone dimly through the thin clouds
—resembled nothing so much as a poor
wash-drawing in some black pigment; the
street-lamps and glowing windows appearing like pin punctures in the paper through
which the light struck brightly. Out of
doors it was rawly cold, but in the great
bare room in the particular building already
mentioned, up the broad, easy steps, and
beyond the double doors, the huge stove
seemed fairly to quiver in its circumambient
heat, to tremble in such ripples about its
ornamented crest that you might have been
justified in forgetting that it was a solid
thing at all, and easily pardonable in im-
agining that it was impalpable—it looked
so like such a monster as some ironmonger

who had dined too heavily might be likely
to encounter in a nightmare. The high, barren room was not unpleasing, though hardly
inviting, being one degree less unattractive
than the waiting-room of some large railway-
station, which, indeed, with its long, wooden
seats and inrailed office, it somewhat resembled. It had but two occupants. Well
within the immediate and torrid neighborhood of the stove—the untutored savage
would have imagined it the presiding deity
of the place and instantly prostrated himself before the inrailed idol — sat a man
tipped back in his chair, with his hands
clasped behind his head, and his feet on
the shining brass barrier that was intended
to prevent the incautious from burning themselves. Another, younger and evidently of
less consideration, stood at a high desk
writing vigorously.

"Wouldn't ha' had such a quiet day if
'twant such a bad one," said the man at the
stove, as a stronger gust of wind than usual
surged against the pane.

His companion nodded acquiescently and
turned to what looked like the ordinary

ledger of the ordinary clerk. But if you
had glanced over his shoulder you would
have been a little surprised if you had only
expected to behold the commonplace en-
tries of ordinary mercantile transactions,
for the building was known as Station-
House Number 1 of that Precinct, and
the book open on the desk was the "blot-
ter" bearing enumeration of malefactions
and crimes blacker than the ink that in
harsh, dry phrase recorded them. On
these pages were kept an account of man's
debit with evil, and on each leaf appeared
an entry of a life's bankruptcy. With the
pitiless, business-like brevity of an invoice,
men, women, and children were described
and despatched—whither? It seemed as if
in that devil's day-book no form of man's
baseness lacked mention ; as if humanity
at no stage of its downfall lacked unworthy
representation, for from the vagrant woman-
child to the drunken beldam, from the
thieving boy to the murderous madman—
all were there.

The decent, trim, regulated aspect of the
place affected you almost with a sense of

uncomfortable unnaturalness when you knew where you really were, admirable though it might be in itself and pleasing in any other connection. What in a hospital would have unqualifiedly won your praise, here seemed incongruous. There was a cold-blooded, matter-of-fact acceptance of evil conditions, and a practical, painstaking preparedness for it that was almost repulsive. It did not seem, despite the humanitarian, that those walls intended to restrain the assassin and the robber should be finished with the spotless plaster and the unstained wainscot of a museum; that these floors, across which reluctant criminals had been dragged, should be swept and tended like those of a public library.

The man by the stove — he was in the undress uniform of his shirt-sleeves — stretched his strong arms and expanded to the full his capacious chest. He did not look a particularly sympathetic person; his experiences could hardly have been such as to render him particularly susceptible to pity, though his face was not bad, only somewhat coarse and heavy. He

was evidently about to address another
remark to his companion, when one of the
doors of the main entrance opened slowly.
A round head from which the hat had
been removed, covered with tight-curling
black hair, was thrust cautiously in, and
the bright black eyes in the fresh, good-
humored, boyish face glanced quickly about
the room.

" Be the rules sthricht," said the new
arrival with a strong Irish accent, " agin
comin' in ?"

He had addressed the man at the desk,
but receiving no answer he apparently
took silence for consent, if not invitation,
and pushing the door a little open, he advanced confidently a step further, still retaining, however, his hold upon the big
bronze door-knob. He was a young fellow
of about twenty-two or -three, with that
peculiar look of intrepid alertness that a
young Irishman more than any one else
possesses, the fact that he was an Irishman being discoverable at a glance. The
perfection of his physical condition was
clearly shown by his firm skin, now red-

dened by the wind and rain. Though he
was rather under the medium height, it
was evident that his well-formed limbs
were vigorous and sinewy. His legs were
covered with tight corduroy, worn and
shiny, and around his throat was loosely
knotted a bright-colored handkerchief.
Nowise abashed by the forbidding morose-
ness of the two occupants of the place,
he again looked easily around, and then
glanced for an instant out of the still open
door.

"'The invitation's not as pressin' as some
ye give," he said, "but I'll not stand on
ceremony with ye, an' just step in."

"What d' you want here?" asked the
man at the desk, seeing that the other dis-
dained to speak.

"What would a man be wantin' here?
Yer company, d' ye think?"

"Ye'll get nothin' else, an' too much of
that if ye don't clear out," answered the
other, who was evidently a compatriot, but
one of longer residence in America.

"Ain't this the station-house?" asked the
young fellow aggrievedly.

" Ye'll find out that it is."

" Thin I'd loike to know av it's not here that a gintleman that's timporarily out o' imployment and consequintly not possessin' the wealth av a railway Crasus can find accommodation for the night."

For all response, the man addressed jerked his chin out sharply.

" It's here I've been given to understand that the government—good luck to it, an' may it nade a voter whin I am meself a citizen—provides lodgins for thim that calls for thim in a quiet, paceable manner; an' that bein' so, considerin' the circumstances I have mintioned, I'd ask the favor of a room. The place is not iligant, but dacent, an' I make no question."

"Come in and shut that door," growled the officer at the stove.

" An' I would, but I'm not alone," replied the applicant. "Would ye have me shuttin' the door in the face of a lady ?"

Dropping his feet to the floor, the policeman who had last spoken turned to gaze at the intruder in wonder.

" I'll bid her, with yer lave, to come in,"

said the young man; then turning he called into the outer darkness, "Norah, Norah, me dear, ye may come up."

He held the heavy door full open, and a young woman came in with a rush, the wind forcing her skirt as well as the light shawl which she held over her head into bulging folds. She was not more than eighteen, and as she stood brushing the rain from her hair that fell shaggily over her forehead she was with her frank, unpretentious beauty a sufficiently charming picture. Plainly, tidily clad as she was, there was evident in her dress that self-respecting coquetry that a pretty woman in any station always finds means to exhibit in any material, and her face, beside its prettiness, was honest, wholesome, and intelligent. She glanced timidly from one of the strangers to the other, and then moving closer to her companion she took his hand in her own.

"Me wife," announced the young Irishman proudly. "Mrs. Moichel Casey."

She dropped a little courtesy to each of the officers—first to the "door-keeper" behind the desk, and then, in some way divin-

ing that the other was of higher rank, she
turned and bobbed a deeper one to him.
Standing hand in hand, she with a certain
blushing diffidence and he with an air of
careless confidence that had nothing about
it of impudent assurance ; both young and
evidently free from all conscious or purposeful evil, they were a strange pair for
that sin-haunted place.

Accustomed as the burly captain was to
all the varying degrees and complexities of
human malefaction, this unexpected apparition of insouciant innocence astonished and
confused him ; even the door-keeper prepared to listen, for he carefully wiped his
pen and placed it in the little iron rack. In
that place a murder of the most atrocious
character would hardly have caused a stir
of interest, but this was certainly something new. Whining vagrants who had already appeared as criminals had been seen
there by the score; decrepit age, vicious
indulgence, imbecile ignorance, all at one
time or another had been given shelter
beneath that roof; but always, in all who
had applied for such protection, clearly and

4

plainly could be seen adequate cause for such appeal.

" I know," continued Mr. Casey, " that the place is respectable though the company is bad, an' I do not hesitate to bring me wife here."

" Mike," whispered the young woman re- monstratingly, " the gintlemen moight think that ye meant thim."

" Hush, me darlin'," he answered ; " sure they'll see I mane that it's the company they kape."

As the old police-captain looked more closely at him, his experienced eye detected that the natural gayety of the youngster's nature and nation was very slightly but still artificially heightened.

" An' this, thin, is the station-house," he continued. " I niver before saw the inside of it—whin I go out of that door may I in- ter it for the last toime—but many of me frinds, I make no shame to say, is inti- mately acquainted with it. Norah, me gurl, it's your work, that it is. Whin ye have shinin' before ye two bright eyes, it's little that the sparkle of a single glass 'll attract ye. I've been a sober lad, gintlemen, iver since the toime I see me gurl. I'll not say much o' what I was before, but I was young thin and wild. The divil—may he be sus-pinded by his own tail so as all the harm he can do will be in the reach av his hoofs—was strong in me, an' though his riverence did the best that he could for combattin' him, it was no avail. That was in the ould country; for I was born in the county Sligo before I came here."

" You're a west-of-Ireland man," said the policeman.

"That an' no other," answered Casey, who had at first looked from one to the other of the officers, but now addressed his remarks exclusively to the captain. He was a middle-aged man, and not at all the kind of a person whose thoughts, a word, a voice, a face, would easily start down the wreck-strewn road of memory. But, for some reason, at the moment some force cracked the slowly-harden-ing heart-crust. Perhaps it was the influ-ences of the day, for no true Irishman feels quite the same on the 17th of March as on

any other day of the year, especially if he
has been born on the troubled and troub-
lous island. And the captain had been
born there long, long before; in resurgent
strength he remembered suddenly and without apparent cause the rude cabin almost
lost in the landscape—so small, so shape-
less, so like in color to the soil around it that
it might readily have been taken for some
accidental elevation of the earth; he remembered the swarming children, the mis-
cellaneous animals; he recollected many a
homely detail and many a trivial fact; and
then, his thoughts taking erratic bound, he
recalled how, when he was between child-
hood and boyhood, he had watched the
glowing sunset, with the smoke curling thin-
ly and bluely up against it, over in the west,
whither he had been told that the friends,
neighbors, and relatives whom he had seen
depart, singly and in families, were gone,
and he had wondered if the skies were
always as bright in the daytimes of that
other and wonderful world.

"It's there I lived till a year this very
toime, sor. But it was not there that I first

saw Norah. It was here in America—while
the feelin' of loneliness was still on me, that
I found her — here in America where I'd
come to make me fortune — where I expected to pick up goold, an' where I found
a jew'l. The fortune 'll come. When ye've
got love in yer heart, there's no room for
fear or even for hope, an' all waitin's a joke,
seein' you don't wait for that. Ah, but it's
a hard toime we had. The ould folks were
agin me from the furst; but Norah, from,
the swate day whin she called me an impudent thafe that no dacent gurl would spake
with, never deserted me."

"Mike," said his pretty companion, "the
gintlemen may not be carin' to hear all
this."

"If I wear your patience as smooth as me
corduroys, perhaps, sor, ye'll remember the
toime yerself whin yer heart could make the
journey from yer throat to yer boots and
back agin quicker than ye'd say the saint's
howly name, jist at the distant sight of a
thrim shape."

He paused as if for an answer, but receiving no response, unless the quick con-

traction of his chief listener's shaggy eyebrows might be considered one, he continued :

"They were agin me, an' the since of the
situation was with thim, I'll confiss. What
a gurl loike Norah Roach could want with
a useless crayture loike Mike Casey no one
could see. I'll grant that; I've felt loike
breakin' me own head for its presumption
in thinkin' av it. But a gurl, sor, should
be let to have her own way. The Lord's
given her those bright eyes for somethin',
an' she can see farther into a human heart
than father or mother, whose sight's oft a bit
blurred with age. An' Norah looked into
my heart, an' seein' her own image there
came back, as well she moight, to her own
lookin'-glass to take another peep."

"Mike," said the girl, "it was on yer
bended knees that ye besought me to listen
to ye."

"Sure the more easy that I might kiss
yer little hand, seein' yer lips was not allowed me thin."

A blush—no faint, incipient flush, but a
heavy, honest wave of color — crimsoned

the girl's face as she pettishly withdrew her hand from his.

"They were agin me from the first, for they had in their minds a great marriage for her—a man who owned siven dump-wagons and eighteen horses. But she'd niver look at him, even with his velvet waistcoat and goolden chain. If he had been a crayture av any sperit—as it was there was nothin' I could do with him. I have been acquainted with men," continued Mr. Casey, reflectively, "who would not fight sober, but I niver saw a man but him that would not fight drunk. There was nothin' to do with him at all. The ould folks was agin me; the praste was agin me; all was agin me; me own past was even agin meself. I had only me love for Norah to spake for me, an' I made the most of me single frind. Whin she'd jump out av the cabin window on the summer nights and mate me by the willows on the bank av the canal, she saw I loved her and she trusted me—God bless her!"—and his hand now sought hers— "an' here we are in spite of all with love in our hearts."

It could hardly have been the day alone that affected the listener, for he thought now how he himself had once stood in almost the same situation, when he with his young wife, who had since died, had landed at Castle Garden with only the money for the day's support about him ; and long as it was ago—a daughter was now teaching in the public school a block away—he lived again in that old time.

"What happened ?" he asked, in a gentler tone than the door-keeper had ever before heard.

"Little enough. Norah would not go agin the expriss wishes of the ould people, an' so she sid at last that she'd marry the man on a certain day fixed."

"Well ?"

"Well, she sid so."

"How comes it then that—"

"Oh, that's what's botherin' ye, is it ? Don't ye see if the pore gurl was ready an' willin' to do what they wished she couldn't do more."

"Certainly not, but—"

"If the marriage could not take place, she bein' ready, small blame to her."

"But—"

"If the man niver came, how could she be marryin' him? An' he niver came, thrust me for that. Some of the b'yes got hold av him an' fixed him illigantly, an' thin to make the matter more sure, they nailed up his doors and windows till the fiend himself could niver have got out. Shure how could she marry him, an' she so dutiful to her parents?"

The captain smiled grimly.

"So thin, havin' done all in her power to plaze the family, she just shlipped out av the same window to plaze me, an' I may make bowld to say to plaze herself."

"Rafferty," said the captain, turning to the man at the desk, "we can lodge these people for the night?"

"Yes, sir."

"Take the fools, then, and do what you can for them." Rafferty, followed by his charges, started for the door, through which they all disappeared, with a short scrape of the foot and nod of the head from Casey and another courtesy from the young wife. For a moment the sound of their steps could

be heard on the hard floor as they sought
the inner recesses of the building, and then
the silence of the room was only broken
by the ticking of the big clock and the occasional splutter of the electric light.

Presently, however, the voices of some
persons advancing rapidly along the corridor reached the room, and the door leading
to the regions beyond was thrown hurriedly
open. Rafferty and the young man entered
in animated discussion.

"Let me spake to him," said Casey, excitedly. "Ye cannot kape me from spakin'
to him." Then stepping briskly across the
intervening space, he again stood before the
astonished officer at the stove.

"Jist a little look here wan side, if ye
plaze," he said, persuasively.

With a docility such as the door-keeper
had never witnessed the puissant and dread-
ed captain of the First Precinct allowed himself to be led into a corner, and consented,
at first carelessly, to glance at and then to
read carefully a small bit of paper that Casey
drew from an inner pocket and held before

his eyes. The subordinate, who was watching the scene with absorbing interest, saw his superior look quickly at the young fellow, and then, after a laugh that ended somewhat abruptly, turn from him and walk across the room.

"Rafferty," he said, as he wheeled about, "take these people and treat them, as near as we are able, as if they were in the best hotel in town. D' ye understand?—break every rule we've got if they want it."

Speechless in his wonder, the obedient Rafferty led his now triumphant opponent through the same door by which they had entered.

The clock ticked on, and the light, after passing through a sputtering and purple eclipse, shone forth steadily for some time. After a while Rafferty again returned. As he entered he glanced at the officer he had left behind, and found that he had resumed that attitude at the rail that he must have adopted with his citizenship. Crossing the floor silently, the door-keeper sought his former place at the desk and prepared to go on with his work. Hardly, however, had he taken up his pen when he was startled by an unwonted sound. He looked up astounded. Could it be true? In all the years of his experience in the place he had never known such a thing. His superior was actually singing. At first low and doubtingly, and then louder and more surely, in hoarse, cracked voice, he was humming to himself the refrain of some song. The listening man at last, with fresh amazement, caught the words of the rudely rendered melody:

> " But there's nothing half so sweet in life
> As love's young dream."

It was so the words ran.

Rising, the elder policeman went to the window, against which the rain had begun to beat violently, and, drumming on the pane with his fingers, proceeded to whistle the simple air.

" Rafferty," he said, suddenly turning to his subordinate, " all the fools in the world aren't dead yet."

Rafferty looked dubiously at his pen.

" What do you suppose those two young idiots have done?"

Rafferty's imagination was unequal to the demand made upon it.

"By—," began the captain, and then suddenly stopped short. "They were only married this afternoon. That was the certificate he showed me. They are on their wedding-trip, do you hear?—and the first night of it they're spending in the station-house."

Rafferty gazed at his superior as if he had expected him to laugh, and was surprised to find that he did not.

Turning again and looking out into the darkness of the night, the captain hummed once more between his teeth, in a voice as hoarse as that of the rising wind,

"No, there's nothing half so sweet in life
As love's young dream."

"A MAD WORLD, MY MASTERS"

Two o'clock in the morning,
January 1, 189–.

As this journal will never be seen by
other eyes than mine, I shall write with
more than the autobiographic frankness of
Benvenuto Cellini, of Jean Jacques Rous-
seau, of Anthony Trollope. I will not be
guilty of that highly-praised form of hypoc-
risy, that senseless aberration, that is called
modesty. I possess unusual, even strangely exceptional, mental powers. I have always found that I could easily comprehend
the natures of all persons whom I have
really known, understanding their every action and often anticipating their very words,
and I can only think that what I comprehend I must contain, and that, therefore,
mine must exceed all other intelligences. I
do not know that I should make any boast

5

of this, for, in truth, the intellects of those
I have encountered—and I have met many
of the most famous and respected men of
my day—have not been of a nature to excite my admiration.   Sooner or later I have
discovered the idiosyncratic derangement
marring the symmetry of the mind.   Everywhere I have found men possessed of some
mental defect, guilty of some unreason—
mastered by love, driven by hate, embit-
tered by envy, deluded by vanity, sunken
in superstition, restless with ambition, eager
in faction.   I view with amazement and
horror the state of mankind.   The world,
seen beneath the calm, clear light of pure
reason, appears to me to be suffering from
universal dementia.   But why use a palli-
ating word?   Why not recognize the fact
in strong, familiar English?   The world is
mad.

I do not wonder that I am what is called
a successful man.   I do not wonder that I
am envied, flattered, feared.   My only astonishment is that I have not accomplished
more—not acquired unprecedented power—
not won unexampled wealth.   I know that

I possess wide influence and a great fortune, but with my exceptional abilities I
should have done more. I am so strong
and mankind is so weak. I am so practical
and all others so visionary. I am so sensible and the rest so irrational. Search, try
as I will, I can find no inexplicable desires,
no unreasoning prejudices, no such ignorant
credulity as I have discovered in all with
whom I have been brought in contact. I
can discern no such eccentric offshoots
from concentric self.

I am aware that I have much, in a material way, that has been and is of great assistance to me. I have always been very
rich, receiving a large fortune from my
mother — my father's first wife. This I
have nearly doubled, so careful have I
been in its investment and expenditure.
My half-brother, Edward, has often remonstrated with me about the time and
thought I give to every dollar I spend, saying that I already had more money than I
wanted.

"You are so rich," he has said, almost
contemptuously, in his strange, impulsive

fashion, " that you might squander a penny or two now and then."

" What do you call rich?" I asked, trying, as I always do, to bring him directly to the facts of the case; "can any one be too rich?"

"He is rich," he answered instantly, "who need only work for fame."

I shook my head sadly, for I wished him to understand that I disapproved of such false, misleading generalities. I am always deeply grieved when I find him so fanciful, so inaccurate, so deluded.

I have entered public life and have held several important offices. I did not do this from any foolish, unpractical ideas, such as I often find in young and inexperienced men. I took up politics as I would any ordinary business enterprise. I found mismanagement, corruption, and ignorance on every hand. As a citizen—as a member of this joint-stock company bearing the name of the United States — I thought that it would be wise for me—a large holder of its stock—to look into the conduct of its affairs. I might in so acting serve as an example

for others. Such examples are, indeed, sadly
needed. My friends, when by chance they
speak of public matters, allude to those
occupying official position as a gentleman
might to the steward on his estate—as a
person something above a servant, possibly
a very worthy being, but certainly not an
equal. And I wish to say here that I firmly
believe that the aristocracy of America is
the most careless and luxurious that has
ever existed since society took form, for it
is the only one that has been unwilling to
exert itself to the extent of undertaking the
hitherto honorable occupation of governing
—a right for which other aristocracies have
given battle—and consented to pay others
to do it.

When long ago I told Edward what I intended to do, he merely laughed at me.

" Why should you trouble yourself about
this patch-work of a country? Politics, they
say, is a game, and success in American
political life depends, as it does in our na-
tional poker, only on luck and ' bluffing.' "

I did not attempt to answer him. Perhaps it would have been better had I al-

ways argued each point, and at any cost of
time and labor brought him to see reason.
I fear I have humored him too much.

I am not greatly liked. At this, however,
I am not in the least astonished. Any one
so evidently superior as myself must necessarily be exceedingly unpopular. My position and reputation are in themselves awing,
and my manner is not one of familiar gayety.
The fact is, I must confess, not displeasing
to me. I am not sorry that the meaning-
less jest halts on the tongue and the heedless laugh is stilled at my approach. It is
part of the homage involuntarily paid to
my great mental elevation. I am aware
that people even avoid me. This, too, is
only natural. What can vain trifling have
in common with serious purpose ? At a
ball, whither I had unwillingly gone, I
heard one young girl speak some words to
another that I think as clearly as anything
express the feeling with which I am regarded.

"Your great man is too ponderous," she
said, ignorant of the fact that I was close
behind her, "like the pious Æneas and the

'blameless king' of the race of Mentor and
of Imlac. He has all the dulness of a calm
and all the terrors of a tempest. I would
as soon talk agnosticism to the Archbishop
of Canterbury or nihilism to the Czar of
Russia as address an average society remark to him."

Such, in brief statement, is a summing up
of my character, possession, and position as
I stand on this winter's night at the beginning of another January. As this period
returns I always endeavor to strike a trial
balance, as it were, with myself; and now,
having reviewed my present situation, I
feel competent to enter upon these coming months.

To-night we have, as it is called, seen the
old year out and the new year in—a pro-
ceeding apparently necessitating much ri-
diculous and inane frivolity. Edward, my
half-brother, was, as he always is on such
occasions, the chief promoter of the evening's levity, most ably assisted by Edith,
who, I must say, brought unfailing help to
the execution of any proposed and preposterous plan. At dinner there were only

Edward, Edith, her father, and one or two
others ; but during the evening many friends
came in, and when the clock struck twelve
we formed a goodly company. We all stood
silent while the last stroke trembled away,
and the pealing of the city's bells came to
us through the open window, now loud, now
low, on the bitter winter wind. Edith had
drawn the curtain about her as a protection
against the cold and stood listening. I saw
Edward look at her. Was it a revelation?
Edith blushed quickly, deeply, and looked
down. Could he for an instant think of
asking her to marry him? Would she for
an instant entertain the idea? Remembering his poverty and hers, it would hardly
seem probable. Still, I know too well the
real imbecility of this boasted winner in the
"competitive examination" of evolution—
man—to believe it impossible. My position
may, indeed, become difficult and perplexing.

January 9, 189-.

To-day Edward regularly took up his residence in my house. Since the loss of his
money—the loss !—rather the absurd and

"EDITH HAD DRAWN THE CURTAIN ABOUT HER."

criminal surrender of his fortune to the creditors of the firm in whose bankruptcy he was legally only partially involved — since that time we have had much talk as to where he had better go, and finally I asked him to live with me until something could be definitely arranged as to his future. Our conferences have necessitated his constant presence in the house, and I have recently seen more of him than I have at any time since we were boys. I have watched him closely, and I have discovered, among other things, that his attentions to Edith are greater than the mere exigencies of society demand. I fear that in his impulsive, unthinking way he has allowed himself to fall in love with her, as it is called—a phrase that on its face shows that humanity at large has some remote appreciation of the undesirable and lowering nature of the condition, for it directly implies that the state is not voluntarily entered upon, but that the unfortunate has heedlessly stumbled or "fallen" into it.

A stronger contrast than the one existing between my own character and that of

my half-brother could not well be found.
My calm, equable temperament has always
been sharply opposed to his wild, extravagant, enthusiastic nature. His passionate
joys and griefs have always been wholly
inexplicable to me, but now at last I fear
I have learned the true, sad cause. Even
when we were boys—when we were little
more than children — I remember that I
was often amazed at his want of self-con-
trol. I recollect that when I was about
twelve years old and he several years
younger I was astounded at the wild ex-
cess of his grief at a very trivial incident.
A litter of puppies that we owned together
was one day accidentally destroyed. For
a whole day Edward refused to eat, and it
was a week before he recovered his accustomed gayety. Through the contempt I
felt for such weakness, even at that early
age, I am sure I was strengthened in that
moderation for which I have always been
celebrated. Remembering his extravagant
conduct on that occasion, I cannot but feel
that if any sorrow should come to him now
when years have brought him no greater

power of self-command, but rather greater
laxity of will, the result might indeed be
lamentable.

January 17, 189-.

Since Edward has been living with me I
have followed his movements closely, and
discovered much to cause me uneasiness,
even alarm. He spends a great part of
the day with Edith — a waste of time he
clearly cannot afford. They talk, they
walk, they read, they paint together. I can
no longer doubt that he will soon, if he
has not done it already, ask her to become
his wife. Whether she would consent I cannot now say. She is not an unusually silly
girl, and I think would hardly commit the
inexcusable folly of accepting a man who
is absolutely a pauper. I cannot, indeed,
believe that she could become the victim of
that strange and fantastic madness that is
named love. I cannot think it possible,
but every day my confidence in the rationality of all around me becomes less and
less.

I have always believed that a marriage

between Edith and myself would fulfil every reasonable requirement.   She is young, handsome, of excellent family.   I am a man of settled habits, established reputation, and above all, large wealth.

January 22, 189-.

To-day I had a long talk with Edward about his future.   I have often, since the loss of his money, pointed out to him that it would be necessary for him to do something towards his own support.   I must confess that he has always, and much to my surprise, readily acceded to what I have said.

For some time I have been looking for some suitable occupation for him, and yesterday I made up my mind to offer him a subordinate position in a mill in which I have a large interest.   I laid my proposition before him this afternoon, and to my utter amazement found that he was unwilling to accept it.

He told me that he was determined to become an artist.

For an instant I was too astonished even

to answer, but quickly realizing that I must
at once turn him from his folly, I told him
plainly what I thought.   While he was in
possession of his fortune, he was at liberty,
I said, to amuse himself with any unre-
munerative occupation he saw fit, but now,
I pointed out, his altered circumstances
necessitated real, practical, strenuous exer-
tion.

" I can support myself," he replied.   " I
may even say more.   I believe that I can
make myself known."

I told him that this was merely visionary,
or at best problematical—that a certainty
is as much better than a hope, as a fact is
better than a doubt.

"A certainty," he answered, losing himself in one of his constantly recurring fits
of blind enthusiasm, "has always been the
enemy of success.   Genius is courage.   I
might lead the life of a torpid fool in your
little spinning village, eat enough and drink
enough, and in time, when the senses were
through with me, die and be buried.   Would
one state differ materially from another
— would it matter whether I were above

ground or below? Would that dull accu-
mulation of scarce animate years be worth
an instant of struggling, hoping, fearing,
despairing existence? Living is striving,
and striving is living. I would rather, at
any time, live under the inspiring influence
of a glorious possibility than under the
deadening depression of a tame assurance."

I argued with him, but to no purpose.
This strange infatuation has taken strong
possession of him, a possession too firm to
be shaken by words. He must be tried by
incisive fact before he can realize his folly.

This new freak will probably cause me
much trouble and expense. He says he
would rather starve in a garret than give
up this—the cherished purpose of his life.
He protests that he never will accept a
penny from me. I wish I could have some
faith in the strength of his resolution.

January 26, 189-.

I am very much disappointed in Edward.
Putting my desk in order to-day, I found a
note written to him that had, in some way,

gotten among my papers. On the back of
it were scrawled some rhyming lines.

[A number of verses, evidently the ones
mentioned, were found in the journal, upon
a loose note such as is described, and are
here inserted.—ED.]

Dreaming, although it is day,
    Drowsily stretched on the grass ;
Letting my wits run away ;
    Letting realities pass.

Drowsily stretched on the grass ;
    Building up castles in air ;
Letting realities pass ;
    Free from the turmoil and care.

Building up castles in air ;
    Lazily lying at rest ;
Free from the turmoil and care ;
    Wasting my time, they protest.

Lazily lying at rest ;
    Blinking away at the sun ;
Wasting my time, they protest,
    Since there's so much to be done.

Blinking away at the sun ;
    I wish them luck on their way.
Since there's so much to be done,
    I shall have nothing to say.

I wish them luck on their way.
　　If they but leave me to dream,
I shall have nothing to say,
　　False though the vision may seem.

If they but leave me to dream,
　　Dreaming that you could love me ;
False though the vision may seem ;
　　Dreaming what never can be.

Dreaming that you could love me ;
　　Dreaming, although it is day ;
Dreaming what never can be ;
　　Letting my wits run away.

Could anything be more preposterous,
more wantonly reckless, more heedless of
all obligation?   I did not expect to find
the firmness of purpose, the recognition of
practical considerations, that are part of a
strong character; but I certainly did not
expect to discover such a shameless repu-
diation of all the duties of life.

February 2, 189–.

My mind is made up.   Reason demands
that I should ask Edith to marry me.   I
must do this, if for nothing else, in order to
save Edward and herself.   I cannot but

think that my duty to my kind, and the dictates of that natural religion of humanity that teaches us how much we owe to those who are to come after us—the great positive belief—command me to do all in my power to prevent their union. I firmly believe that her reason is mastered by that strange frenzy—love. If I do not quickly interfere, she may fulfil the promise that I believe she has already made to Edward and become his wife.

To-day I took the first step towards the accomplishment of my purpose. I went to her father, an aged clergyman, who had been one of my father's most intimate friends, and asked his consent to address his daughter. He received me with evident constraint. I have always suspected that he disliked me.

"She is a good girl," he said, "and I trust her fully. If you obtain her consent you shall have mine."

"My dear sir," I answered, "I want more than your consent. I want—I fear I need —your assistance."

"I am not one to advise a girl in a mat-

6

ter of this sort. The free, natural, unrestrained impulse is the best guide."

"But," I almost interrupted, "this is not
merely what is called an affair of the heart.
I am a serious, practical man. I am very
rich. I can give your daughter all that she
desires. In short, every conclusion of com-
mon-sense must tell you that I am the
proper husband for her."

"I know," he replied, reluctantly, "that
you offer every worldly advantage, and for
her sake I am doing what I never did for
myself. I am remembering purely worldly
things. She has known you all her life. If
she can love you I shall be glad that so
many of the good things of this life should
be hers."

"What has this thing that you call love
to do with it?" I asked, almost impatiently.
"I can do for her what few others could
ever hope to do. If she married Edward,
for example, as I sometimes suspect she
thinks of doing, she would be subjected to
a life of self-denial and perhaps even of
physical discomfort. It is our duty to save
her from herself."

"I am glad you have spoken of your brother," he quickly replied. "I have, indeed, sometimes thought that her heart was given to him, and, unfortunate as such a marriage would be in a worldly way, if she really loves him I cannot, I dare not, oppose it."

"Why not?" I asked, hardly concealing my disgust at such absurd sentimentality.

"I might be responsible for her future unhappiness—even for her eternal misery. A single error may harden the conscience and work irremediable evil to the soul."

"Do you wish your daughter," I asked, with some warmth, "to give up the real advantages I offer her for an absurd fancy?"

"Love is God speaking in the world, and none dare disobey His behests," he replied, solemnly. "Self-seeking and avarice, like all other vices, once admitted to the heart, turn traitors and let in their allies. It is only by watchful resistance that we can hope to save ourselves—to attain the glories of the life to come."

"And would you renounce the present, the actual, the almost tangible good for

the vague blessings of a problematical future?"

"Like Kant, I give up imperfect knowledge in order to make room for perfect belief."

I did not argue with him. I have his
permission to urge my suit with the daughter. That is all I sought. I hope that she
may be more reasonable than the father.

February 6, 189–

I become more and more anxious about
Edward. At times he is moody and de-
jected to an unusual degree, and again he
is unnaturally, feverishly exhilarated. When
Edith is not present he seems to lose all interest in what is going on, and only on her
reappearance does he exhibit any signs of
real attention.

February 15, 189–.

I have spoken to Edith at last.

I drove out with a large party to skate
on a lake which lies near the town, and
in the afternoon I told her what I have
for a long time purposed to tell her. It
happened in this wise. After an hour or

so on the ice Edith, I noticed, became tired
and seated herself on a rock on the shore
from which the snow had been blown by the
wind. I paused at her side, and the rest
soon passed on. The sun was just sinking
over the brim of the valley, and the shadows of the hills fell long and dark over the
snow-covered country. Gleams caught from
the flaming sky shone on the ice, and a thin
new moon hung low before us. A perfect
stillness was over all, broken only now and
then by the faint, far-away laughter of the
skaters taking one more turn before depart-
ure. I do not note these facts for the reason that they had any such effect upon me
as I have found described in some of the
few romances that curiosity has led me to
read, but rather for the purpose of record-
ing that I was entirely free from such ex-
traneous influences. I was as calm and
collected as if I had been buying a ticket
at the dullest and dreariest railway-station
in the country.

We were alone. The time had come. I
determined to make one last, logical appeal
to her reason.

"I have," I began, "a proposition to make to you, and I ask your earnest consideration of it."

She turned her eyes, which had been fixed on a light that had just twinkled into being on the opposite shore, in astonishment upon me.

"I wish to ask you," I continued, "to marry me. Do not answer at once. You will, I am sure, on reflection find that for every reason it would be wise for you to do so. I am not old or ill-looking, and I certainly have distinguished position and immense wealth."

She seemed to regard me with steadily increasing apprehension—almost with terror—and when I paused she shrank from me and answered hurriedly,

"I must ask you not to say this to me. I cannot listen to you."

"Why not?" I asked.

"I thought you knew   You should know. I am engaged to your brother."

Although I was not in the least surprised at this announcement, I did not reply at once.

"That need not necessarily make any difference," I said, finally. "It is not now too late to correct the mistake you have made. I imagine that you have acted from impulse. I believe that upon reconsideration you will readily see the error into which you have fallen. You will realize how absurd, how insane, such a marriage would be. You will probably tell me that you love him. I make an appeal to your better reason. Try and free yourself, at least for the moment, from this misleading fancy. Is it wise to throw away all that I have to offer —wealth, position, power—for a transitory whim? Is it not better, wiser on the whole, that you should at once break this unreasonable engagement and marry me?"

She again looked far away at the light on the opposite shore.

"Do not speak to me," she said, suddenly. "You do not remember who you are— who I am."

"Is this reason?" I asked, patiently.

"No," she answered, "it is not reason. It is something beyond reason. Honor transcends reason. I am engaged to marry

your brother. You have no right to speak
to me—I, none to listen to you."

I need make no comment on this strange
interview. Poor thing, so blind, so weak,
so unreasoning. I can only pity, I cannot
blame her.

February 17, 189-.

Edith's mother has heard of my proposal
for her daughter's hand, and is doing all
she can to aid me. If it were not for nu-
merous proofs of mental weakness that I
have discovered in this maternal being, I
should believe that she was a person of uncommon sense. As it is, I must conclude
that this is only an accidental and unusual
manifestation of rationality.

March 3, 189-.

I saw Edith again to-day. She was much
quieter and apparently less unsettled in her
mind.

My position is certainly perplexing. Not
for a moment can I believe that I should
consent to her marriage with Edward. If
for no other reason, it would be my duty to
break off the engagement on account of his

unhappy state of mind. As yet with an infinite cunning he has managed to conceal
his infirmity from every one but myself, and
I hesitate to reveal what has hitherto been
unsuspected. I shall let all go on as it is
until I am compelled to act. Rather, however, than have her marry one who is insane,
I will tell the truth.

March 8, 189–.

I am rarely at a loss how to act under
any given circumstances—indeed, I can recollect no occasion on which I was not able
promptly and effectively to meet the exigencies of the moment. I am glad that I
have the clearness of mind to perceive instantly the proper course to pursue, and
the strength of mind to act in accordance
with my perceptions. I am especially glad
at this present time, for if I had not this
power of instantaneous decision, I should
not have known how to carry myself in the
scene through which I have just passed.

I received a note from Edith this morning,
asking me to see her, as there was something important about which she wished to
speak to me. I did not quite like to be dis-

turbed.   My agent was making his month-
ly report, and it is excessively annoying to be
interrupted when busy.   I supposed that she
wanted to tell me that she had concluded
to accept me as her husband, an announcement that could as well be made at any other
time ; but, on the chance that she really had
something urgent to say to me, I dismissed
the man and hurried across the lawn to her
house.   As I entered the room I saw that
she was greatly agitated.   She paced the
floor excitedly, and I noticed that her in-
tertwined fingers worked nervously.   After
a moment of hesitation she came and stood
close beside me.

"I do not want any one to hear," she almost whispered.   "Come with me."

She was dressed to go out, and without a
remonstrance I followed her through the
hall to the gravel walk before the house.
It was a raw, cold March day, and the
black branches writhed under a strong wind
against a heavy, slaty sky.

"Come," she commanded.

I followed her to the street.

"I can tell you better here," she said.
"We shall be alone and not alone."

I did not understand her.

"You did me the honor to ask me to become your wife," she continued. "I consent."

"I think," I replied, "that it will not be necessary for me to express my gratification. I must say, however, that I believe that you have decided for the best."

Still, she did not pause or offer to turn around. I could not understand why so simple an announcement should be made in so melodramatic a manner, and, impatient to return to my work, I suggested that, as the day was so unpleasant, it might be wise to defer our walk until another time.

"I have not told you all," she answered, with a strange mingling of terror and despair. "Cannot you spare me a few moments of your valuable time?"

I told her that I was very much occupied, but if she had anything really of importance to tell me, I could listen to her without any very great inconvenience.

"I think the subject is one to which you will be willing to give your attention," she answered, contemptuously, "I wish to speak of money."

"Ah!" I exclaimed, delighted to find her
so rational. "This is indeed a pleasant
surprise. I cannot, at the moment, give you
all the detailed information that you would
undoubtedly wish in regard to my fortune;
but I will at once have an exact statement
drawn up and laid before you—"

"No," she cried, the growing scorn in her
voice displacing the last trace of fear. "You
cannot understand me. How could I expect that you would? I wish you to do
something for me — something unusual—
something—" she paused. "I wish you to
give me some money."

"Why?" I asked, with a calmness that
I felt must have some effect, excited as
she was.

"I cannot tell you."

"In a money transaction—" I began.

"If you trust me to the extent of asking
me to become your wife, cannot you trust
me in this?"

"It may be for the very reason that you
are to become my wife that I now wish to
know."

I saw that the reasonableness of this

made some impression on her. She walked for a few moments without speaking, her eyes fixed on the wet and shining pavement, for the rain had begun to fall in fine particles which the wind blew coldly in our faces.

"Suppose that there are reasons—" she began, hesitatingly, "reasons involving others, that make it inexpedient, impossible even, for me to speak."

"I cannot think," I answered, "that I should be acting judiciously in giving you, an inexperienced girl, money without knowing what you intend to do with it."

"If you do not give it to me—only twelve hundred dollars," she said, with sudden fierceness, "I withdraw my promise."

"Is this wise?" I asked.

"I must have the money," she exclaimed. "Give it to me. How can you care for me enough to marry me if you are willing to see me suffer?"

"This is irrelevant," I answered.

"Must I tell you?"

"Would not that be the simpler and wiser way?"

"If I must do it—" she began, and then breaking off. "You are a man of honor—"

"I believe I may say," I corrected her, "that I am a man of sense."

"You are a wise man—a great one, some say—you will see that what I tell you must be kept a secret. I want it for my brother. He has been led away—he has been weak —he has," she said, coming closer to me, "forged!"

In the street as we were, she buried her face in her hands.

"And you wish this money in order that the crime may be condoned?"

"Yes."

"Do you not think that it would be far better if the law were allowed to take its course? He—"

"It would kill my father."

"Undoubtedly such a disgraceful affair must cause much pain, but, after all, would it not be best that he should be placed where he can do no further harm?"

"Save him this once," she cried, "and you will save him forever."

"Possibly," I answered, "possibly."

"Give me the money," she said, with an intensity of which I did not think her capable. "It is a matter of bargain and sale. I will have my price."

I consented. I may have done wrong, but I consented.

That the end justifies the means, is one of the soundest deductions of perfect wisdom. In its deep import it far exceeds in value any other sentence in which the world has summed up its experiences. If I have made an error in judgment it will be the first, and indeed if I have I possess this consolation : I have been led to it by no unworthy influence. I have done as I have because it has seemed to me most judicious.

April 5, 189-.

Since Edith has promised to become my wife I have noticed a change in her manner to me. She still treats me with what appears to be utter loathing, but nevertheless with a certain painful deference. She is silent, listless, sad. She speaks as if she were repeating a lesson, and will hardly for an instant look at me. Our engagement is

not yet announced, but it will be in a day
or two. I am glad that all has come out so
satisfactorily. If the world would be guided
by the commonest of common sense how
different life would be.

April 7, 189-.

On the whole, I do not know whether to
be glad or sorry that a mind of such an uncommon order has been given to me. I do
not know whether to be thankful or regret-
ful that the sequential action of natural
forces has given me abilities of such a kind
as to remove me even from all sympathy
with my fellow-men.

I seem possessed of the limitless intelligence that apprehends all — of the calm,
pure reason that permits no stain of doubt
—the utter consummation and perfection of
intellectual power. I feel as the keeper of
a mad-house must often feel. Like him I
must always be on my guard, lest I forget
the afflictions of others and lose my temper
at their unreasonableness. I must manage,
cajole, and deceive.

I am weary.

Sustain me, divine reason—that reason

that dwelt in the brain of Plato and, in
other mode, guided the understanding of
his great opposite, Aristotle; that reason
that fled the madman of Macedonia at the
temple in the Egyptian sands, but accompanied that sanest of men, the Roman con-
queror, from the Rhone to the Tagus; that
reason that remained with Socrates even
in his last hour, but in later time deserted
the arch-cynic of Ferney at the supreme
moment; that inexplicable power that led
Kepler to his mighty laws and Newton to
his grandest truth, and in our own day
stirred the systematizing intellect of Dar-
win; that element in the gray matter of
the brain that drove the steam through the
throbbing piston, that set the first type side
by side beneath the groaning press, that
sent electricity along the trembling wire;
that ineffable quality that brings order out
of chaos, and points the way through the wil-
dernesses of sophistication—divine reason,
may your saving grace ever remain with me,
and may I always be blessed with your sus-
taining presence. Keep and protect me
from all noxious influences, but chiefly pro-

7

tect me from myself, lest in some moment
of weakness I forget your wondrous name
and go hopelessly astray.

April 11, 189-.

I have just had a terrible interview with
Edward.   His madness, which has hitherto
been apparently harmless, has assumed a
new and violent aspect.   I am much disturbed by this new development and hardly
know what to do.

The immediate cause of Edward's excitement was the announcement of my engagement to Edith.   He came to me as I sat
in the library, and demanded in agitated
tones if what he had heard was true.

I told him briefly and calmly that it was.

"It is not her fault," he exclaimed; "they
have forced her to it.   I have not been
allowed to see her for days.   They have
driven her into this hateful bargain."

"On the contrary," I answered, "all has
been done with her full consent; indeed, at
her own request.   You will soon see, I hope,
that everything is better as it is.   You are
very poor.   I am very rich.   There can be
no doubt as to the wisdom of her choice."

He replied wildly, in furious, almost incoherent words. I waited patiently until he paused.

"I can, of course," I said, "understand that you think that you have suffered an injury in being deprived of Edith. I should be willing to make up to you in any way I can your loss. What—"

I do not think I ever saw a person so completely submerged in the tumultuous floods of unrestrained passion. He would not listen to me. In action and in word he was indeed a maniac.

I feared even for my personal safety.

"Stop!" he cried, "this is too much. I have endured your insults long enough. I have suffered long enough through your cold and supercilious nature. I know what acts you are willing to commit in the name of reason. I have heard your cant. I know your calculating selfishness, your stolid cruelty, your unbounded meanness. I know your heart, untouched by humanizing sympathy—incapable of love, unequal even to hate. I know you. I know you as you really are. I will do all that I can to prevent this marriage."

I grieve for him. It distresses me to see so fine an organism as the human mind so thoroughly ruined.

April 13, 189-.

I have determined what to do. I have sent for a celebrated physician—a specialist, an alienist—who will give his opinion about Edward and tell me whether it is quite safe to allow him such absolute liberty.

April 15, 189-.

To-night Dr. Varley dined with Edward and myself. I thought that during the dinner the physician would have an opportunity of studying my brother's case. It is best that Edward should not know that he is the object of our solicitude, for that would only excite him the more. The talk this evening, as I expected, was unrestrained, and the doctor had every opportunity of noting Edward's mental failings. My brother was as extravagant and irrational as he always is, and what he said presented a strange contrast to my simple, logical discourse.

I saw Dr. Varley glance from one to the

other of us with evident and constantly growing interest. In the course of the evening I drew him aside and asked him what conclusion he had reached.

"This recent trouble," he answered, hesitatingly, "of which you tell me has certainly had its effect upon him."

He glanced sharply at me. That he wished to spare my feelings and withhold his opinion until he had further opportunity for examination was evident.

April 16, 189–.

How can I write what has happened? My hand trembles so violently that I can hardly hold my pen. Just now Edward desired to see me. I received him as usual in the library. His voice when he first spoke was hoarse with passion, and I could with difficulty understand what he said.

"At last I know the truth," he exclaimed. "It came to me after our last meeting, and since then suspicion has changed to assurance. I should pity you, but I cannot. I have only remained in your house to watch

over her, over you — to save her, to save
you.   Give her up, and I will be silent.
Keep to your purpose, and I will denounce
you to this man whom you yourself have
brought here and who seems blindly ignorant of—"

He must in his raving madness have attacked me, for the next thing that I remember was seeing him lying on the floor pale
and still, with the blood trickling from a
wound in his head.   In defending myself
I must have unconsciously done him some
injury.

I hurriedly summoned the servants, and
saying that Mr. Edward had met with an
accident, sent one of them for Dr. Varley.

The physician is now with him.

Strange—strange and sad that the swift,
strong, sure action of the brain should ever
be so weakened.   Pitiful that this wonderful mechanism should ever go so wofully
awry and, as in the breaking of powerful
machinery, work death and destruction.

It is a warm spring evening.   My window is open.   I hear people on the veranda.   They are talking.   What do they say?

How strangely sensitive to sound I am.
Their voices, distant as they are, come to
me with great distinctness.

They have moved, and I can hear even
more clearly.

Some one says that Edward is not seriously hurt.

Now they say—what? That I attacked
my brother and sought to kill him—that I
am the madman, and—

[This journal having come into my possession, I have thought that I might vent-
ure to publish portions of it. It is very
long. As there is much in it that does
not bear upon the history of these three
lives I have omitted many things, but I
think I have retained enough—absolutely
unaltered—to maintain a consecutive nar-
rative.—ED.]

"GUILTY SIR GUY"

"GUILTY SIR GUY"

"—that affable familiar ghost."
Shakespeare's Sonnets, lxxxvi.

"And you have all that any one could wish," said the guest after a dinner that could only become a memory and never an indigestion.

"Possibly," murmured the host, mournfully. "Possibly."

"You should be the happiest man on earth," continued the guest.

"Ah!" sighed Mr. Chisholm, the host, looking his friend sadly in the face. "You little know the trials of a man to whom money is no object at all."

"No," admitted his companion. "I do not. I would willingly, I think, undergo them. The amount of moral discipline to be derived therefrom must be very great. They must be irksome, but improving."

"You do not approach appreciation of my meaning," answered Mr. Chisholm, dismally. "With only your millions you can still be a comparatively contented man. But pause—beware."

"You alarm me."

"Do not let them increase. You can still long for something that money can buy, and hope in time to call it yours. I cannot. With my absolutely unlimited means there is nothing purchasable that I cannot obtain. Man, however, is so made that he must always wish for something more. I can only wish for what money can never bring me, and therefore my case is hopeless."

"It is very sad," said the friend.

"If I can't talk freely to you—my oldest friend—a friend as long ago as when gold was over two hundred and fifty," said Mr. Chisholm, impulsively, "I can't to any one. My trouble is largely of a family nature."

"Indeed," responded the friend in a tone that could readily melt into one of deep commiseration, but would not be entirely inconsistent with one of genial depreciation.

"I have apparently everything that the heart of man can desire." Mr. Chisholm glanced across the broad terrace, down the smooth-coated lawns, to the river, where the dark outline of his trim steam-yacht stood sharply against the broad waters purpling beneath a sunset sky. "But I am wretched. All is spoiled for me by one miserable fact."

"Yes," softly murmured the guest.

"I have no false pride and no false shame. I know that an American is only a person who has forgotten that he is something else. I know that as an American I am no more expected to have a pedigree than a Spanish grandee is necessarily expected to have a fortune. I am troubled purely on æsthetic grounds. I miss above all those appurtenances that are only to be had in any real perfection by inheritance. Mine is no vulgar discontent." He paused for a moment. "I have the finest place in the country. But there is no mystery, no suggestion about it. It is

new. It is crude as a fact and down-
right as a dollar. I saw the first stone
of the foundation laid and the last Bougue-
reau hung. Everything about me is new.
I myself am also new. I've too much the
crudity and crispness of a fresh greenback.
I am unable to escape from it. I seem
condemned to a world where everything
is freshly polished and there are no corners off. I have bought several baronial
halls in England, three or four châteaux in
France—all places where I need not have
feared to find the varnish sticky. But it
was no use. I couldn't stand the contrast.
I did not correlate, so to speak, with the
Van Dyck portraits, and was utterly thrown
into the background by a crusader's armor.
I had at last to give up. It is extremely
unpleasant for a man to feel himself put
down at his own fireside by a piece of his
own furniture."

"Excessively disagreeable, I should imagine," said the friend.

"And so I always come back here, where
there isn't even a candle-snuffer to humili-
ate me."

"The finest modern villa residence in the world."

"There it is again," said Mr. Chisholm, in despair. "Villa residence! It might be a stucco house with a tin fountain in the front yard. Villa residence! I'll burn it to-morrow."

"My dear friend," said the guest, anxiously, "restrain yourself. You are excited."

"Who wouldn't be excited? All has been done that money can do, and the thing's a failure. I haven't even a haunted room in it."

"A haunted room," repeated the friend, slowly. "You think that you would be satisfied with a haunted room?"

"I am quite sure," answered Mr. Chisholm, "that I could get on with that. It would be extremely grateful to me to have ghostly footfalls on the terrace and hollow groans on the front stairs, but I could be happy if I only had a haunted room."

"It might," said the friend, blowing a cloud of cigar smoke into what seemed to Mr. Chisholm's excited imagination a tolerably accurate representation of a trunkless head with snaky locks, "it might perhaps be managed."

"No," ejaculated Mr. Chisholm in awed surprise.

"I think that really it might be arranged."

"Do that," cried the host, bringing his closed hand down on the table with a bang that made the gold service rattle, "and I'll never forget it."

"I should not be in the least surprised," answered the friend. "One can never tell what may come of introducing a ghost into the house."

"Do not trifle with me," said Mr. Chisholm, with deep feeling. "If you do not really think that it can be done, tell me at once. Do not keep me in suspense."

"But—"

"Do not think of the cost," interrupted Mr. Chisholm, excitedly. "In a matter of this importance the expense should not be considered. Besides, a ghost is a fancy article and should command a fancy price."

"It isn't so much," responded the friend,

"the cost of the original article as the duty that makes them so high. It has always been the policy of our government to protect and encourage the production of native ghosts, but hitherto such endeavors have met with very slight success. There have been a few produced in New England— witches and the like—and the negroes in the South have some crude, savage, clumsy apparitions, but that is all. It is a fatal mistake. The American people will never be able to turn out really good, original ghosts until there is a popular demand, and the only way to create that demand is to educate the popular taste by the importation of really excellent examples. Take off the duty on ghosts, I say, and in a few years the American-made spectre can challenge any world."

"I'll send to Europe for a ghost immediately," exclaimed Mr. Chisholm.

"You need hardly go to that trouble," answered the friend, reflectively. "I know a man who keeps a little shop downtown and imports a low class of ghosts. Perhaps he might have something really good.

8

At least it would be worth your while to
try him."

"Why doesn't he bring over the best
quality?"

"There is absolutely no call for the best.
The most of his customers are mediums,
and they are satisfied with a very poor line
of goods."

"Do you think he is a responsible party
—could be trusted not to put you off with
a modern imitation?"

"I have always understood that he was a
very worthy and respectable person. His
father was in the business before him, and
I myself have had some dealings with the
son that gave me perfect satisfaction. I am
sure that he could get you a nice, respectable family ghost on comparatively easy
terms. He keeps an agent in Europe, and
I have no doubt that he often picks up a
good thing very cheap."

"Where does most of his stock come
from?"

"I believe that it is largely gathered on
the Continent. The old families are breaking up, sales occurring every day, and I

understand that a good judge of the article
—a man that knows a ghost when he sees
one—can sometimes get surprisingly good
bargains.   Latterly some English ghosts
have come into the market, but they are
rare as yet."

" I should want the very best."

" Then I unhesitatingly advise you to
get an English one.   There is nothing like
an English ghost for quality and design."

" I hope," continued Mr. Chisholm, anxiously, " that there will be no failure.   It is
rather important for me to have the blue-
room haunted just now.   I'll tell you all
about it."

He drew his chair closer to his companion and coughed slightly.

" You know," he began, " that when we
were on the other side there was a young
Englishman—the Duke of Westendington—
rather attentive to my girl.   It was all in
the newspapers, and you must have seen it.
Well, he's coming over here to get my consent to marry her."

" I congratulate you," said the friend.

" On the whole I suppose you may do

that," answered Mr. Chisholm. " But I
have had a great deal of trouble about this
matter. I supposed at first that all dukes
were alike, but I soon found out my mistake. They vary. They vary just as much
as other things. One duke may be very insignificant in comparison with another. It
is very hard for a stranger to distinguish
these nice shades of difference. Finally,
however, I hit upon a way of setting all
doubt at rest."

" Yes," said the friend, with interest.

" We met a duke as soon as we got over
there, but I was suspicious of him from the
first. He might be all right and again he
mightn't. There was no sort of certainty
about it."

" What was the matter with him ?" asked
the friend.

" I learned that his character was univer-
sally respected, and that his reputation was
absolutely unimpeachable. I was very much
disappointed, for I liked the young fellow
exceedingly. But I had to let him go."

" Why ?"

" I couldn't be sure of him. I didn't

know just what his standing might be. You
see he had never asserted himself. A duke
of irreproachable life and with an unstained
reputation was something to look upon with
suspicion. Why, my dear friend, he might
have been afraid to be anything else. Sim-
eon Chisholm was too sharp to be fooled
that way. I gave him up. I was at first
discouraged, but quickly I was given new
hope. I came upon Westendington. He
was everything that I could possibly desire.
None but the real thing could have gone
through what he had and kept out of Port-
land. I made the most particular inquiries.
I was charmed with all that I learned. He
was conceded on all sides to be the most
consummate blackguard that the peerage
had ever produced. He had repeatedly
been discovered cheating at cards—he had
hocussed a race-horse—had brought about
three divorces—had been horsewhipped at
least a dozen times. I took him to my
arms at once."

"'Of course you will give your consent?'"

"Why, certainly. It wouldn't do to miss
such a chance as that."

"But—"

"True," answered Mr. Chisholm. "I
haven't told you why I want the ghost.
Well, when I was in England he asked us
down, with a lot of other people, to Feversleigh Castle, and a fine old place I understand it is. I didn't go. I should have
stood out like a restoration. I believe that
he has a very fine and mysterious ghost
there. I didn't ask him about it, though I
should have liked to do so. I felt a certain delicacy about intruding upon family
matters. Now he is coming here, and I
don't want to be behind in anything. As
it is, I confess I am distressed, humiliated.
I haven't even a dog that howls a warning,
or a raven to croak calamity."

"It is awkward," admitted the friend.

Mr. Chisholm took a sip of the wine
bought from a semi-royal family at a wholly
royal price, and glanced at the scene of cul-
tivated loveliness that lay before him.

"We'll see about this matter to-morrow."

It was about eleven o'clock the next
morning when Mr. Chisholm and his friend

turned out of the great thoroughfare, where
the traffic of the city flowed steadily and tu-
multuously along, into a quiet and seclud-
ed court. The atmosphere—which would
have, perhaps, been invigorating in the trop-
ics or the stoke-hole of an ocean-steamer—
suddenly became cool in the shadow of tall
buildings, and the din was stilled to a low
murmur.

"I should not think," remarked Mr. Chisholm, "that this was exactly the place for a
lively business."

"Well, you see," answered his friend, "the
business is not exactly what you would call
lively. I have advised a place farther uptown, with a ghost against a black velvet
background in each plate-glass window
wringing its hands or tearing its shroud.
That would attract attention. However,
this man seems only to take a sort of virtu-
oso-like interest, and does not care for the
worry and anxiety of anything so exten-
sive."

"It is a great pity," answered Mr. Chisholm; "with a little capital and 'go' it might,
I imagine, be made a very good thing."

" I have always thought so myself. Why,
only a little thing that I suggested the other
day, if skilfully worked, might bring a mint
of money. The trade is always longing for
new ways to advertise. What could be better than to start out a procession of ghosts
through the streets to deliver little *papier-
maché* tomb-stones, with a taking descrip-
tion printed on them of the goods to be
puffed? Or a very neat thing might be
got up in imitation coffin-plates."

" ' Bogle,' " said Mr. Chisholm, pointing to
a sign over a shop-door; "that must be
the place. Yes, ' Andrew Bogle, Importer
and Dealer in Foreign and Domestic Spirits.' "

It was a dark little shop between two
huge warehouses, and the green mould and
crumbling brick showed that the sun rarely
had a chance at it. Glancing in at the
dirty, narrow-paned window, Mr. Chisholm
beheld some broken looking-glasses, a pile
of chains, and a large old hall-clock.

" Something supernatural about every one
of them," whispered the friend.

As they approached the door they felt

the deadly oppression of the miasmatic and
stifling air, broken only now and then by
sudden ice-cold draughts that chilled the
marrow in their bones. Entering the shop,
Mr. Chisholm noticed on one side of the
narrow threshold a heavy beam with a hook
in it, and on the other a curiously marked
plank. He determined to ask their use.
The room was low, dark, and dingy, but the
man who stood behind the counter appeared
a perfect picture of bright, smiling, contented jollity.

"Is that the person?" asked Mr. Chisholm, doubtfully.

"Yes," answered the friend.

"Do you really think he is quite to be
trusted? I don't see the shadow of any
mystery, any sickly wanness, even any deadly flickering of the eye."

"A man must have a strong constitution
or he would break down in this business,"
said the friend.

"Bless my soul!" cried Mr. Chisholm, in
great astonishment. "Why?"

"He has to live so largely with ghosts—
a most confined life—and then the night-

work is very hard. Ghosts, on the whole,
prefer the most unhealthy places, and the
conditions under which it is often necessary
to keep them undermine the strongest sys-
tems. One must be beyond all malarial
influence or else one cannot with safety
take proper care of the spectres that haunt
donjon keeps, willow-walks, and the like.
One must be able to bear the close, impure
air of unopened rooms such as is necessary
for the proper preservation of ghosts that
affect secret chambers, vaults, and tombs.
If you will look at this man closely you
will see that the insalubrious nature of his
employment has already begun to tell upon
him."

"It is then absolutely necessary to pre-
serve ghosts in their own atmospheres?"

"Absolutely. If it were otherwise they
would become so hale, hearty, and substan-
tial that no one would look at them at any
price. The sanitary arrangements always
have to be very imperfect."

During this conversation, which had been
carefully carried on in a low tone, the proprietor of the establishment stood smiling
and rubbing his hands.

"Well, gentlemen," he said, in a jovial voice, "what can I do for you?"

"Mr. Chisholm—" began the friend. "By the way, you remember me?"

"Perfectly, sir, perfectly," answered the shopman. "You bought, about two months ago, a spectral hound for your country-place, to scare away the tramps. I sincerely hope that it gives satisfaction."

"It worked perfectly at first, but I am afraid that they are getting rather too accustomed to it."

"I've heard the same complaint from other parties," answered the man, "and I'll tell you what I'll do. I'll give you a liberal allowance for the hound, and let you have one of our headless horsemen, of which we sell a great many to people going into the city in the winter, or leaving their country-places in the summer to go to Europe. They have been found most efficacious."

"I'll think about it and let you know, but I've brought a friend who wants a quiet family ghost for himself. I told him that you would be sure to have just the thing."

"I flatter myself," replied the dealer,

with some severity, "that the establishment is too well known to require any puff-
ing on my part. We can furnish anything,
from a brownie to amuse the children to a
cavalcade of mediæval knights for the in-
struction of the adult—all warranted and
the best in the market."

"Mr. Chisholm is furnishing a new house,
and wishes a ghost for the blue-room."

"Ah!" exclaimed the man, and his face
shone with gratification. "Who has not
heard of Mr. Chisholm! This is indeed a
commission that gives me great pleasure.
What you wish is not intended strictly for
use. You desire merely an ornament—a
superfluous but aristocratic appendage."

"Exactly," answered Mr. Chisholm.

"This excites the artist in me," exclaimed
the shopman. "Is your house of any particular style or time? I would not like to
commit an anachronism."

"Composite American," replied Mr. Chisholm.

"Then we are quite unrestricted."

"Absolutely."

"If you will just step into the dark

room," said the man, "I will show you some choice things."

"Before you go," observed Mr. Chisholm, "will you kindly tell me what these are?"

He pointed to the beam and plank by the door.

"This," answered the dealer, running his hand affectionately along the rough board, "goes with a ghost that I can show you. This is the beam he hung himself on, and from which in the ghostly state he appears suspended. The effect as a whole is singularly awful. We had the walls torn down and the rafter brought away."

"Wouldn't any other do as well?"

"We try to be accurate in the slightest detail. Now, here was a case where we tried to get along without the real thing, but it would not work. This," he continued, caressing the plank, "belongs to an apparition that wails over a blood-spot. You see the spot there. When the ghost was sent over they thoughtlessly omitted to pack up the blot with it. The consequence was that the ghost was practically useless. We

tried it over a crushed-strawberry stain,
but couldn't get a wail out of it. We were
compelled at a great expense to procure
the original spot. His Serene Highness,
the former owner—in whose family the spectre had been for centuries — knew that he
had us in a tight place and put up the
price."

"Really," said Mr. Chisholm, "this is
extremely interesting."

"We see a good many queer things in
our business, as you may imagine," said
the man. "But will you just step this
way?"

He opened a door between two large
safes, one of which was marked "Œtin-
ger's Essences," and the other "Lucretius's
Superficial Films."

Mr. Chisholm started violently as a large
rocking-chair that stood behind the counter
began, apparently without visible cause, to
rock violently.

"That," said the dealer, noticing the
sudden movement on the part of his customer and following the direction of his
gaze, "is the only American ghost that I

have in stock. It's an old lady who rocked herself to death in colonial Massachusetts. No one will have her on account of her unpleasant habit of predicting the direst evils on every possible occasion. It is annoying and even alarming when you are not accustomed to her. She minds the shop when I step out for a minute, and lets me know if a customer comes in."

Motioning Mr. Chisholm to precede him, the shopman held open the door. The two customers entered a low, dimly-lighted hall at the end of which was a hanging of dark cloth that evidently concealed some opening. They had not taken more than two or three steps when they were startled into a sudden halt by a slow succession of blood-curdling groans. Their tongues clave to the roofs of their mouths, and their knees trembled under them.

"Pardon me a moment," said the dealer, and suddenly disappeared.

With blanched faces Mr. Chisholm and his friend gazed one at the other. The groans were not repeated, and almost immediately the proprietor of the place stood beside them.

"It's only that old idiot from Vampire Hall," said the man, impatiently. "He's very old and garrulous, and I cannot always restrain him. He once frightened a very valuable but new customer into a convulsion."

"Could you — could you," asked Mr. Chisholm, uneasily, "manage not to leave us again? I am afraid that I might accidentally do some harm."

"Not the least danger, sir," answered the man, confidently. "Our goods are not exactly perishable. Why, you walked slap through a ghost a minute ago and didn't know it."

Mr. Chisholm involuntarily jumped.

"Will you step in here and take a seat?" continued the shopman, drawing back the curtain, and pointing into a large, barren room.

The visitors disposed themselves in two stiff-backed chairs, and their conductor suddenly turned out the single gas-jet that had dimly lit the place.

"What did you do that for?" asked Mr. Chisholm, sharply.

"You couldn't possibly judge of the

goods by that light. Some of the shades are very illusive."

"Well," said Mr. Chisholm, discontentedly.

"As I understand, you want a simple ghost that will appear at regular intervals and at a certain place. You don't want anything erratic or fancy. You wouldn't like one that would burn its hand on the furniture or predict your own death?"

"No," answered Mr. Chisholm, hurriedly; "I don't think that I should care for that kind."

"So I imagined," continued the man. "The first apparition that I am going to show you is very old. So old that I doubt if you will like it. You will wish something lighter and less severe."

Gradually the darkness at one end of the room seemed to lose its density, and slowly, as if from a central point, a cold, wan light spread and spread sufficiently to enable a tall, spectral form to be seen. What teeth Mr. Chisholm still possessed chattered violently, and here and there a hair stood erect upon his head. He saw the fig-

9

ure of a monk with cowl drawn forward
over the face, barefooted, and with a pil-
grim's staff. Slowly the apparition moved
along, but at the third step paused and,
throwing back his hood, gazed fixedly at
Mr. Chisholm with eyes that were now cold
and fishy, and now burned like molten glass.

Under the steady look Mr. Chisholm
trembled in every limb.

"We got him from a monastery in Spain,"
said the merchant, glibly, "and he is so
very ancient that really there is no record
of his particular grievance. As his tongue
is cut out, he cannot inform us himself."

"I think," murmured the millionnaire,
"that I should prefer one that could speak.
It might be more companionable."

"I hardly thought this would suit you.
Still, it is in very severe good taste. I'll
show you next a German spectre that might
take your fancy."

The dealer clapped his hands, and the
monk vanished with a suddenness that
made Mr. Chisholm wink. With the despatch of a "lightning-change artist" a
shadowy crusader in vaporous armor ap-

peared. Mingling the sustained tone of a
hoarse bassoon and the plaintive tremolo
of an unlatched gate, the spectre uttered a
few words in a language that neither of the
visitors understood.

"It's Old German," explained the owner.
"He says, 'I did not kill him. I did not
kill him.'"

"Doubtless," said Mr. Chisholm, with a
great assumption of ease, "some unhappy
being who in life was unjustly accused of
crime."

"No. Not at all. That would be quite
in the style of a modern ghost, but these
veritable antiques are quite different. They
are not troubled with the morbid sen-
sitiveness of a later time. I happen to
know this ghost's history. His lament is
that he fell himself into the oil in which he
was about to boil his enemy."

"Take him away," cried Mr. Chisholm,
in unconcealed disgust. "I wouldn't have
such a thing about the house."

"Shall I show you next," asked the man,
"a German polter-geist, a Scotch wraith, an
Irish banshee, or a Dutch spook?"

"Don't you think that I had better have one that speaks English?"

"I was about to suggest it myself."

With a low wail, that for an instant stopped the beating of Mr. Chisholm's heart, a slight, shadowy figure of a woman floated into view. Her delicate young face was as the face of one distraught with grief, and as she moved along she wrung her hands. As she grew more distinct, it could be seen that she was dressed in widow's weeds, which made her countenance appear pale and waxen.

"She murdered her husband," observed the shopman. "Listen."

"The color of it! The color of it!" moaned the spectre.

"Ah!" cried Mr. Chisholm, with a strange creeping of the flesh. "Can—can she mean the—blood?"

"No, no," said the shopman, "not in the least. She finds that black is not becoming."

"I do not think I care for her either," observed the millionnaire with some decision.

"Business is not very good in July, and

I have not as many varieties as I should
like to show you. I have sent away a good
many of my best examples to the country
for the summer, to gain pallor and weakness
in various quiet and unfrequented grave-
yards. Still, I believe I can supply you with
what you want. Would you like to see the
'Horror of Ghoul Hall,' or the shrouded
skeleton from Goblin Chase? Or would
you care to have a look at Lady Bleightly's
ghost, that only appears thrice in a century
and then generally reduces the beholder to
a gibbering idiot? Ah — yes — I have it
now. Sir Guy de Varquier, a nice, gentle-
manly apparition of the very highest distinction."

"There is nothing unpleasant about
him?"

"Very subdued, and calculated to satisfy
the most fastidious. He is very anxious
that his former abode should be kept secret
—a matter of family pride."

"Bring him on," said Mr. Chisholm, resignedly.

A sickly, dull red glow shone in the darkness which had been allowed to gather, and

as it increased there appeared the dim
figure of a man in a dress of the time of
the "Merry Monarch." In his right hand
he held aloft a wine-glass, and from the
ruby liquid that it contained there streamed
a flood of heavy crimson light.

"Drink — drink — drink !" moaned the
ghost.

"He does not seem unamiable," observed Mr. Chisholm. "What was his difficulty ?"

"Ask him," replied the dealer.

"Sir Guy de Varquier," began Mr. Chisholm, unsteadily, and with evident uncer-
tainty as to the proper mode of address, it
being the first time that he had ever spoken
to a ghost, "what—"

"Beg pardon," answered the spectre, abruptly, "we don't pronounce it that way at
home. We pronounce it—Veryqueer."

"I am sure," said Mr. Chisholm, politely,
"I did not mean to hurt your feelings."

"Hurt my feelings !" repeated the ghost,
in some surprise. "Why, I'm an Englishman."

"Might I ask," continued Mr. Chisholm,

anxious to change the subject, "why you carry this wine-glass?"

"That is what makes me unique. There is absolutely no other ghost who carries a wine-glass. I am called 'Guilty Sir Guy.'"

The spectre paused expectantly, but Mr. Chisholm could only ask clumsily,

"Why?"

"You have never heard of me?" said the ghost, in evident astonishment. "But I forget your misfortune. Still, I have haunted several Americans who have been stopping at our place. Indeed, it was from an American that I first got the idea of coming to the States."

"Yes?" said Mr. Chisholm, questioningly.

"He offered to take me 'starring' in my own car through the country. His idea was to give Hamlet, and make the ghost the leading part."

"You did not accept?"

"No. A De Varquier an actor! Never. I am perfectly aware that persons who appear nightly upon the stage are now received by the very best people, but I have

no sympathy or patience with the levelling
tendencies of the times."

The ghost sighed deeply.

"It may appear strange to you that I
should be willing to let myself out in this
way like a green-grocer for the evening.   I
would not do it if I could help myself.   It
is a hard necessity, and my pride revolts at
it, but the fact is my tomb is very much out
of repair.   Something must be done or I
sha'n't have a place to lay my shade.   A
ghost can't always be on the—the haunt.
However, my good friend Mr. Bogle has
promised that the thing shall be done as
quietly as possible ; and as, at my next place,
I shall, of course, assume a new name, it
may not be so bad.   Besides, so many of
the aristocracy have taken to dabbling in
trade, I do not feel this step so much as I
otherwise might.   I have a great deal of
leisure—our place being shut up most of
the time, I have only to be on hand for the
shooting and Christmas—so I thought I
might just as well profit by it."

There was a short pause, during which
Mr. Chisholm vainly tried to think of something to say.

"As you may imagine," continued the ghost, "I am extremely anxious that this step of mine should be kept quite secret. As an old member of the family I naturally have its honor at heart. The honor of most ancient families depends upon its members doing nothing. If what I am doing were known, I fear the moral effect upon the present head of the house. I alone have influence enough to keep him from disgracing the rank he holds. You have no idea of the hours that I have haunted him, trying to make him realize the duties he owes to his order. I am quite sure that he considers me a prodigious bore. I may even say that I believe that he hates the very sight of me."

"But the story," suggested Mr. Chisholm.

"Ah, yes, to be sure, the story," said the apparition. "I loved the beautiful heiress of the Cholmondeley-Chichester-Chortesques. She was betrothed to another. I swore that I would kill that other and drink the bride's health in his blood on the day of my marriage. I did what I swore I

would do. At the feast held in celebration
of our union the butler produced a decanter
containing my rival's heart's blood, which
I had carefully collected and preserved for
the occasion. It looked like a fair kind of
claret. I arose. The glass touched my
lips. I took one sip and fell down dead."

"Horrible," cried Mr. Chisholm.

"'That is the story," said the spectre,
blandly.

"Yes," observed Mr. Chisholm.

"But it isn't true."

"Not true?"

"Bless you, hardly a word of it. I don't
mind telling you the truth, since the story
might prejudice you against me. As a
general thing, however, I prefer to keep up
the mystery. Now, just to show you out of
what beginnings these things grow. All
there was of this was that I forgot my
speech, blushed—and that is the way pos-
terity serves up the incident."

"I am very glad to hear it," said Mr.
Chisholm. "I hope that I may be able to
make it worth your while to remain with
me."

"If the house is dark and the work light I think it might be arranged. You will find me very easy to get on with. I can readily accustom myself to new surroundings. You will notice, for example, that my language is quite modern, and I fear even that I have picked up a few Americanisms. But what can you expect when you are compelled to associate with spirits that only dematerialized yesterday? Why, last week the ghost of a man who had struck a bonanza had the impudence to leave his epitaph on me. However, Mr. Bogle, my agent, will inform you of my terms. I never transact business myself."

The glass fell to the floor and, the liquid losing its luminous quality, the ghost disappeared.

"I'll take him," said Mr. Chisholm, finally. "All things considered, the terms are quite reasonable."

"Yes, sir. Thank you, sir. But before you go I should like to show you a real curiosity. The very ghost mentioned by Pliny the Younger, that appeared to the philosopher Athenodorus. If you have time—"

"Not to-day," said Mr. Chisholm. " I'm really in quite a hurry."

" Some time when you are passing, then," said the dealer, bowing at the door-sill.

Two persons sat upon the terrace over-looking the vast grounds of Mr. Chisholm's summer home. The moon had risen far enough to light the wide spaces of lawn and glisten in a broad band over the great, dark, silently flowing river. It was very beautiful, but the two could see nothing of this. They were seated at a spot where if they had looked they could have discerned only the end of a brick wall and a huge earthen jar containing a spreading cactus. It is hardly necessary to say that they were lovers. It is, however, advisable to state that one was Angelina Chisholm and the other the Duke of Westendington, and that the paternal consent to their marriage had only been given an hour before.

" And now," said Angelina, joyfully, " I can call you by your first name. That is," she added, doubtfully, "if dukes have first names."

"Oh," replied her lover, cheerfully, " I have several. Indeed, I do not know but that I have rather a large assortment. I am called Edward Albert Arthur Lionel—"

"I shall call you Lionel," announced Angelina with decision.

"Why?" he asked, with all the complacent assurance of a lover that, whatever the answer may be, it will assuredly be right.

"It is so nice and dukely," she answered, adoringly.

There was a short pause.

"At last," he exclaimed, "I can escape the life of deception I have been compelled to lead so long. At last I can be myself."

"Yes," she answered, sympathizingly; "you need not pretend to be a wicked villain and a vulgar ruffian any longer. You can be your own good, upright, exemplary self."

There was a short pause.

"When I heard of poor Chippendale's fate—that your father would have nothing to do with him on account of his excellent reputation—I was in despair. I knew that, if anything, I was more objectionably good than he, and the terrible thought came to me that if Mr. Chisholm were to know the truth he would distrust me and his doors would be closed to me forever. It was some time before I made up my mind. But, my resolution once taken, I acted immediately. I managed to have tales of my utter moral depravity, every one of them false, brought to your father's ears. I managed to make him believe that I was the most abandoned scoundrel in the kingdom, and then — happiness — I obtained his permission to see you."

There was a short pause.

"But after that why—why did you remain silent so long?"

"There was a terrible reason. I was not free. I could not speak of my love until I was sure of one thing. The family curse —"

He sprang to his feet and paced the terrace nervously, while she shrank trembling into the corner.

"Even now we may not escape it. I think I have arranged all, but I may be mistaken. The curse that has blighted so many of the marriages of my family — for it was especially pronounced on marriages —may yet descend and involve us. Are you willing to trust me?"

"I am! I am!" she cried.

There was a long pause.

"To-night," she said, as they parted, "you are to sleep in the haunted chamber. If—" she hesitated, "if the ghost should be disappointing or shouldn't happen to appear at all, I hope you will not mention it to papa. He is very sensitive about this and might be displeased."

"Never," he exclaimed, "will I tell him what did not happen."

There was a short pause.

It was midnight in the blue-room.

It would be quite proper to add that the clock had just gone twelve and that the candle had expired with a sickly flicker. But then it would not be true. The fact was that the big clock on the stairway, after striking twelve as clocks sometimes do at midnight, had just finished playing one of

Waldteufel's waltzes, and the electric light shone brilliantly.

The Duke, who was sitting by the window smoking, suddenly heard a voice at his elbow.

"Turn down that light."

His cigar fell from his trembling hand.

"Why?" he asked, turning round, but seeing no one.

"I can't appear. I can't even see you," the voice replied. "I can stand a candle or a gas-burner or two, but this electric light literally puts me out."

"You have come to haunt me?"

"I grieve exceedingly to thrust myself upon you, but really I am not my own master. I am only fulfilling my duty. That is what I am here to do. It is very unpleasant for me to frighten people out of their wits."

"Then you are very frightful?"

"I would undoubtedly terrify you very much. But if you refuse to turn out the light, why, I have done my part, and—"

The Duke felt that the ghost had shrugged its shoulders.

"I really must, though," he said to himself resignedly, as he thought of Angelina's
warning and remembered that Mr. Chisholm might question him in the morning.

"It would really," said the spectral voice
give me great pain to make you imbecile
through fear."

"I must see you," answered the Duke,
"so draw it as mild as you can."

He touched a button and the room suddenly became perfectly dark. The ruby
light appeared. The spectre was slowly
shadowed forth.

"Drink, drink—" the ghost began, and
then suddenly paused in evident embarrassment.

"What," said the Duke, straightening
himself up and taking a step forward—
"what are you doing here?"

The ghost coughed nervously.

"You see—" it began.

"Now this won't do at all," continued
the Duke, angrily. "Why are you over
here? I thought I left you at Feversleigh
Castle where you belong."

"I imagined that, you being away and
10

nothing needed, I might just run over to see the country. I—"

"Nonsense. I know better. I have heard the whole story. You have sneaked off here in your own interest. And after all you have said about '*noblesse oblige*.' I say it is disgraceful."

"Believe me," said the now thoroughly humiliated spectre, "all I have done was for what I thought was the best."

"This marriage is everything in the world to me, and you have opposed it."

"Such a *mésalliance*."

"Better than misery."

"I cannot think that I should be doing my duty to consent," replied the spectre, critically. "Good-fortune has brought me here, and if this marriage takes place I shall, however painful it may be for me to do so, pronounce the family curse."

The Duke sank trembling on his knees.

"I must," said the ghost, now again himself and seeing his way out of an awkward predicament, "uphold the dignity of the family at any cost."

"No, no," gasped the terrified man in

hardly articulate tones, cold drops of per-
spiration starting out upon his forehead.

" I really must," replied the ghost. " I
had to do it when the third duke married
Peggy Thistlecraft, the actress, and you know
how unpleasant all that turned out."

" Spare me—spare me," moaned the unhappy young man.

" But an American," continued the ghost
pettishly. " I know that they are rather the
thing just now; but, after all, that is but another sign of the degeneracy of the times.
These Americans are destroying everything."

" You take all hope from me."

" Oh, you'll get over this little thing.
You think you won't, but you will, and,
what is more, you will be particularly
obliged to me for keeping you from making a fool of yourself."

" Never."

" You'd better have it over the first thing
in the morning and take the noon train for
town."

" Rather than bring the curse on another
I will consent."

" Any one else would have done it

months ago," answered the ghost with that
perfect freedom that family intercourse permits.

"And now if you please," said the Duke,
"could you leave me alone? I find your
presence disturbing."

"A good many other people have also
found it so," murmured the ghost, grimly.

"Leave me."

"I think that when you are fortunate
enough to have me here, and when you have
just profited by my advice, it might be wiser
to listen to me further. My moral support,
at least—"

The Duke turned on the light, and the
spectre was lost in its strong, clear efful-
gence.

"It is very painful to me," said the
Duke, after his interview with Mr. Chisholm
had lasted for some time, "to make the
announcement to you that I am compelled
to make. But the family curse—"

Mr. Chisholm visibly shuddered.

"You have heard of it," said the Duke.

"Yes," whispered the millionnaire.

" It would be launched at once."

" Horrible."

" I thought that I had managed to escape it. I thought that, the marriage once accomplished, all might go well; but last night, in the blue-room—"

" In the what?" demanded Mr. Chisholm.

" In the blue-room—the spirit of an ancestor appeared to me."

" The spirit of your ancestor! The spirit of fiddle-sticks," ejaculated Mr. Chisholm.

" And threatened to utter the—"

" Threatened to utter it, did he? I'll see about his flinging curses around loose."

" Beware. Do not provoke an unknown power."

" An unknown power indeed! Only too well known. Why, that ghost is my own particular property, and a precious bad bargain he is too — the first that I ever made. I was always suspicious of him from the first—he seemed altogether too anxious to conceal his antecedents — and so I put a clever young man of mine on the track. He has just reported to me this morning, and I only just now learned that this ghost came from Feversleigh Castle. But that is not all. With the assistance of our English lawyers, he has made a discovery that I believe will put a new face on this matter."

Mr. Chisholm touched a bell and the clever young man appeared.

"You found that the ghost of Feversleigh Castle, known as 'Guilty Sir Guy,' was not Sir Guy after all?"

The clever young man bowed.

"No!" cried the Duke. "Who then?"

"The family butler," answered the clever young man at a sign from Mr. Chisholm. "He is compelled to go about offering a glass of the wine that he kept for his own use during life to every member of the family in each generation. The generally accredited story has, after the manner of all myths and legends, grown slowly up from this beginning."

"Wonderful!" exclaimed the Duke. "But how did it happen?"

"They were changed at death."

"The butler and Sir Guy?"

"Yes."

"And this is an utter impostor?"

"Utter."

"At last," cried the Duke, "I am free. I must," he continued, in wild delight, "see the true ghost—Sir Guy himself—and get his consent. Of course he'll give it. No one but a low upstart would take advantage of his position. Of course he'll give his consent."

And of course the true ghost did consent.

As the Duke and his young wife were passing through the portrait-gallery on the first night of their arrival at Feversleigh Castle, they saw coming toward them the figure of a tall, graceful man in a costume that De Grammont might have worn. His face was long and sad, but a reckless mirthfulness shone in his long, narrow eyes.

"My children," he said, in a soft, low voice, "be not afraid. I come not for harm, but rather for your good."

Angelina trembled within the encircling arm of the Duke.

"Do not fear, pretty one," continued the spectre in the same silky tones. "There is no curse. It is but the invention of that lying varlet that did usurp my place, and who, methinks, did somewhat overdo the matter. In truth, he did come to regard his tales, uttered after the manner of his kind, as absolute verities."

"No curse?" cried the Duke.

"Young sir, no. I myself, after all, am but an honorary ghost attached to the family as one of some consideration and distinction, until by murder, suicide, or some other peccadillo we are entitled to one. This place that low-born villain did take from me. But I am brought to my own again, even as was his blessed Majesty, and all may now be well."

"How nice!" said Angelina.

"Od'sfish!" murmured the spectre; "if my royal master King Charles could but have seen these Americans!"

IN THE MIDST OF LIFE

Felix Oldys let the book rest upon his knee, with one long, thin finger upon the page he had finished.

"Know then," so ran the words he had just read, "that there are tragedies greater than those that end in death. The extinction of something that cometh from one infinite and seeketh another, and which, while it lasts, is both invisible and impalpable, is a wonderful and terrible spectacle; but in itself it is a happening of but little moment. It only signifies, that is that was before. Wherefore is this lamentable: Man is given here but little time to live and in that time works much evil. Is not this rather the grievous thing, that life should continue, and that the harm, as is the nature of harm, should be without end? Tragedy lies more often in the continuance of life than in its

surcease.   Therefore, I enjoin you, call not
a man's death a tragedy, for, if he had lived,
you know not what evil might have been
wrought.   In truth, were I to write a tragedy wherewith to delight the judicious, for
catastrophe I would take a birth, which is
the beginning of life."

He glanced out of the open window beside which he sat.

It is noon.   Each shadow is reduced to
its minimum.   Since sunrise the encroach-
ing light has been conquering, overrunning
the country, and now its empire has reached
its ultimate extent.   It is noon ; it is also
the year's meridian, for it is July.   There is
not a cloud in the intense, firm sky, and the
heat has grown until the shadeless country
seems almost incandescent.   The day is
perfect ; it is even arrogant in its perfection.   There is the unsympathetic barren-
ness of consummation, the vacuity of absolute satisfaction.   No country could be
fairer, and in no other time could this be
more fair.   Looking as Felix Oldys did
from the window of his library, his eyes
fell upon a wide and grateful scene.   From

the sweep of the drive-way about the house, the ground descends in almost terraced regularity to a small lake; the incline of the valley is so gentle that, though its depth is not great, its opposite slope appears blue and hazy near the rim. The landscape, in its undulant prettiness, seems in the distance a carefully laid out garden, the smooth roads appearing like paths and the regular fields almost like flower-beds. If ever rebellious nature has been tamed, trained, domesticated, almost humanized, it is here. No money, no labor, no thought has been spared, and the whole region is a marvel in its way. Indeed, it is famous throughout the country, and is regarded almost with a certain awe as an Elysium of landscape-gardening into which humanity is translated after having achieved the apotheosis of riches. The house commanding this view is an irregular structure of rough, dark stone, built in such fashion that its outlines follow the contour of the hill upon which it is placed, thus giving it a solidity of aspect that is not without impressiveness. It is very large. There is a high, dim hall, with

a stairway for which a famous sculptor
designed the balustrade; there are long,
shadowy, gilded drawing-rooms, with ceil-
ings painted by a great artist; there is an
impressive leather-decked dining-room and
a gay little silk-hung breakfast-room; there
is a huge conservatory constantly replen-
ished with orchids from the distant green-
houses that glitter in the light like the
palaces of a fairy tale; there are wide-
spreading stables in which are housed
equine perfection in various forms, from
the nimble polo pony to the stately carriage
horse; there are big, adjacent buildings in
which are ranged all vehicles of contempo-
rary or habitual use, from the highest, light-
est cart to the heaviest, most resplendent,
and imposing of coaches. The grounds are
a fit setting for the house. There are broad
lawns dotted with beds as intricate in design and as harmonious in combination of
color as the finest rugs of Teheran; there
are endless walks, sharp-edged and kept
by the gardeners from all blemish of fallen
leaf or twig, in which you might lose
yourself alone; there are trimmed and

tortured groves with cunningly contrived
windings in which you assuredly would lose
yourself with another.

On the whole, it is very costly and very
charming.

The melancholy words Felix Oldys had
read hung persistently in his mind.

In his youth, because of his cadaverous
appearance and the listless, mournful expression of his intelligent, high-bred face,
Oldys had been called the Anatomy of
Melancholy.   There was another reason,
moreover, that justified the appellation.   In
him, as in old Burton's famous volume, was
great store of odd bits of forgotten wit and
wisdom, gathered from the crusted phrases
of dead and long-gone writers—writers often
like the writer of the book he had just laid
down, utterly unknown save to bibloma-
niacal fame.   It was a very small volume
by a certain Sir Geoffrey de Blacquiere,
written with a substrain of melancholy that
one might have been surprised to find—or
not find—in the production of a frequenter
of the Court of the Restoration.   Insignificant though it might be, it was very

valuable, for it was supposed to be unique.
It contained, in the very dissertation that
Oldys had just read, " Upon the Quitting of
this Doleful Habitation," the only printed
account—realistic in detail—of a scandal
about a very great personage, and, having
been rigorously suppressed, this copy was
the only one, so far as known, that had
escaped destruction.   It was bound with
all the art of a Grolier or a Roger Payne,
and was a volume in every way worthy of a
place in Oldys's great library.   It had been
bidden in for him at a recent sale at the
Hôtel Drouot, at a price that had caused his
French competitors to stare at the prodi-
gality of this American millionnaire, as their
forefathers had at the extravagance of some
English " milor."

As Oldys put down the book, he had, at
first, thought only of the sombre meaning
of the passage ; but gradually the mournful
cadence of the words grew stronger, and
he lost the significance of the sense in the
sadness of the sound.

The perfect silence was oppressive—the
silence of a great house—the more notice-

able, perhaps, because one almost insensi-
bly listens for something of the stifled stir
of life in the huge, unpeopled rooms.

Felix Oldys drew out his watch, opened
it, and looked at it. Replacing it, he picked
up his book and settled himself anew in his
chair preparatory to its further perusal.
Hardly, however, had he raised it from his
knee when he let it fall from his powerless
hand.

A woman's quick, wild, piercing shriek
rang through the house.

Starting to his feet, he listened breath-
lessly, motionlessly. In the distance he
heard the noise of hastening steps, a confused tumult of voices. Then, again, there
was perfect stillness. He had hardly time
to recover from the inevitable inactivity
of sudden amazement, and to take half a
dozen steps towards the door, when it was
suddenly thrown open, and a man in the
dress of a house-servant stood before him.

"What is it, Jarvis?" Oldys had time to
ask before the man could collect himself
sufficiently to speak.

"Mr. Daryl has been brought home dead,

11

sir," answered Jarvis, stammering in his excitement. " The horse he was trying over
the gate of the stable-yard fell with him
and killed him. And Miss Annette—"

But Oldys had hurried past him out of
the room.

The light is as intense, the heat as great,
as it was an hour ago when Oldys sat in the
library.   There is not a distinct, severable
sound to be heard ; only the dull, mysterious
hum of a hot summer day as, almost unno-
ticeably, it rises unbrokenly in soft mono-
tone.   There is something grandly restful,
powerfully peaceful, in the time.   Not even
a leaf stirs. Everything is at rest—a lethar-
gic rest; the world seems sunk in narcotic
torpidity.

Suddenly a man appeared at the door
of the house, crossed the veranda, rested
his hands upon the heavy railing, and gazed
intently down the driveway. It was only
an hour since Oldys had let fall his book
to gaze upon that same landscape, but he
looked years older ; it was only an hour, but
it was an hour such as had never come to

him before.   He gazed anxiously down upon
the country, where the white roads showed
among the green fields almost as distinctly
as a chalk mark shows on the cloth of a
billiard-table.   No moving thing was visible.
He shook his head in impatient gesture, his
eyebrows were drawn together angrily, but
under the stiff white moustache his lips
twitched tremulously, weakly.

"God grant they find him," he muttered,
unconsciously.

He is tall and thin; in appearance he is
commanding, even imposing.   He is dressed
in the light, loose garb of summer, and his
clothes are worn with the ease and grace
that mark him as belonging to that small
class who are pre-eminently clothes-wearing
creatures.   In his youth he was hardly
good-looking; in his old age, as sometimes
happens with men of intellectual life, he
has become exceedingly handsome.   Over
his fine old sunburned face is cast a look
of grievous apprehension, almost terror.
You cannot help feeling that it is an unusual expression.   There are some faces
on which sorrow seems to sit naturally;

others on which it appears incongruous,
and as an unfitting and unwonted garment
suddenly put on.   Felix Oldys's countenance had never at any time of his life,
when in repose, expressed much of anything except a mocking but not ill-natured
scepticism.   Now, when he is an old man,
real trouble has for the first time suddenly
found him.   From his father and mother—
both of whom had died when he was too
young to remember either—he had inherited
fortunes which had enabled him to escape
from every evitable annoyance, and an easy-
going and unambitious disposition that kept
him from creating embittering ills for himself.   He had married and had lost his
wife, but the bliss of the holy state had not
been so ecstatic that solitude was unmitigated misery.   His satisfaction in himself
had been absolute, and he had always
thought that he was freed from those human ties that are both the joy and the misery of most.   He had never imposed high
standards upon any one or expected to find
them imposed by others, and the leniency
with which he regarded the world he had

only thought it fair to extend to himself.
He had always been told that he was a selfish man, and as he never contradicted any
one—not even himself—he had always believed it to be so. After his wife's death,
when he discovered that there was still
enough left in the world to make his life
quite as enjoyable as it had been before,
he became more than ever convinced that
he was a selfish, perhaps an unfeeling person. Now, it is with more than a shock
of surprise — it is with something of the
sense of revelation, that he finds that, as
he stands there in the blazing sunlight,
there is some one very necessary to his
happiness.

"On such a morning too," he murmured,
with that feeling that we all have had that
grief is doubly grievous, that it is unbear-
able in its unnaturalness, on some glorious,
brilliant summer day.

The calm - faced, insensitive country is
maddening to him in its stolidity. He
glances at the terrace below him. The
light cane lounging-chairs on the veranda
are in groups, as if continuing the care-

less conversation or perhaps the light con-
fidences of their last occupants, a riding-
crop hangs from the stiff leaves of a cactus;
two tennis rackets lean against a table,
upon which lies a woman's glove.   Everywhere, startling and almost voiceful to
him, are indications of the thoughtless, un-
troubled life of the past—of yesterday—of
the hour before.

"In the midst of life," he said, gently,
recalling words he had caught at some fu-
neral to which he had unwillingly gone,
reluctant always to recognize trouble, and
regarding it as he might some common ob-
trusive upstart who has forced a half-ac-
quaintance.

Another glance at the distant road, and
with lingering step he turned toward the
door and entered the house.

In the comparative obscurity near the
stairway was a group of servants.   His own
man Jarvis stood rather in advance of the
rest, and, as Oldys crossed the hall, ventured
to address him.

"Is he better, sir?" the man asked, hesitatingly, and in the low voice of respectful
sympathy.

His companions ceased their whispered talk and listened for the answer.

"No, Jarvis, no," replied Oldys, absently, and hardly raising his head. "He is still unconscious."

"It's awful, sir," said Jarvis, stepping back.

As Oldys mounted the stairs his feet fell heavily and slowly on the sounding wood; the elastic step, the erect carriage of an hour before were gone. Well he knew the scene that awaited him above; three times he had made the journey from which he was now returning, only to find all practically unchanged. Could he come back to it again without the desired tidings? But Felix Oldys learned, as he had learned that day another thing equally surprising to him, that he was a brave man; and without visible hesitation he opened a door in the upper corridor and entered a large, darkened room.

On the bed lies a young man. His coat is off; his waistcoat is unbuttoned and hangs loosely; he wears white riding-breeches and shining riding-boots, his shirt is widely open at the collar, showing

his short, thick white neck and a little of
the smooth skin of his chest.   In his face is
the apathy of absolute insensibility.   That
he is a glorious human creature is evident.
He is neither tall nor short; neither un-
wieldy nor slight; his head is small, but
finely shaped — the perfectly proportioned
head of the true athlete ; his features are
singularly regular — the line from the first
crisp curl on the forehead down the brow
and nose curving only slightly and in delicate but unfrigid purity.   Bloodless, almost
absolutely white as his face now is, it might
more properly seem the face of some winner in a Nemæan game, almost living still
in the perfect marble of the complete time
before rascal intelligence like a hump-backed
Richard had so entirely usurped the throne,
and when physical beauty was held as
worthy of honor as brains.   By his side,
holding one of his hands, sits a young girl.
If she' had been reared with disadvan-
tageous surroundings and beneath un-
favoring influences, if she had grown up
in poverty and ignorance, she might have
been ugly ; but, born to great fortune and

high position, living all her life in the re-
fining environment that wealth and position generally create, she has to a high
degree that artificial attractiveness that in
our modern eyes is often more desirable
than a more regular but less expressive
loveliness. We have not yet found a word
to describe exactly the quality that we
prize so much. Sometimes we call it "distinction"; sometimes, in attempted explanation, we use the word "interesting";
sometimes all that we can find to say is
that the possessor of this mysterious quality is "nice-looking." One positive, un-
deniable beauty, however, she has — her
dark eyes, which are wide, deep, glorious;
vivid with expression of unthinking, un-
hesitating impulsiveness; intense with assurance of power for self-forgetting, self-sac-
rificing devotion.

She looked up as Oldys entered.

Her face has hardly more color in it
than the face on which her eyes had been
fixed, and a strand of her dark hair which
had broken loose and fallen over her shoulder seems almost to heighten her paleness.

"Can't you see him, father?" she asked in a low, hard voice — a voice dry, desiccated—as if all tears had been wrung from it.

"Not yet," answered Oldys as he wearily seated himself.

"But he must come soon."

"Yes."

"If they can only find him—if they can only find him!" moaned the girl.

"He must surely be at home at this time," replied her father, with the weak assurance of one who speaks only to pacify, and without positive belief in what he says.

"And when he comes do you think he can help him?" continued the girl, with all the unreasoning absurdity of that grief so desperate that even the sound of the words, in which it is impossible that there can be any real comfort, seems to afford relief.

"I understand," said Oldys, as if trying to prove to himself that nothing could be so very bad when he could talk so calmly and collectedly, "that he is considered a very skilful man — quite remarkable, indeed."

"Can't you hear wheels?" she asked again, suddenly looking up.

Oldys turned towards the window, with the impulse that always leads us to look in the direction from which we expect to hear any sound, and listened attentively.

After a motionless moment he shook his head.

" No," he answered, sadly.

The scarce-stirring air, heavy with the perfume of the heated fields, slightly displaced the light curtains, causing a gently-lapping sound and allowing a flickering light to play over the floor.

"And this is my honeymoon!" cried the girl in a rebellious voice, "and I was so happy, happy — unconsciously, unhesitatingly happy. Is that all that joy is—something so that we may feel grief the more? It is wrong to trouble any one so happy as I have been—it is cruel. I might have been spared because I was so happy. Does God see so much happiness on earth that he dared destroy mine?"

" Annette," said Oldys, "you cannot know what you say. You frighten me ; you harm yourself."

"It is right that I should rebel," she went on unheeding her father, her voice now rising, now falling, until it might have seemed to any one too distant to distinguish her words that she was crooning some wild, irregular dirge. "Life is not given to us as a bribe. God may expect gratitude, but not blindness. Such a death as this is outrage — only an exercise of pitiless power. But I will not believe that he will die," she cried, "that he will die and that I shall live. He taught me how to live and now he is dead. Before I knew him I knew nothing; I breathed, I moved, I lay down and I rose up. I called it living, but I did not live. Then he came and all was changed. The most trivial things of life meant more, the commonest aspects of the world gained beauty. It was as if my senses had been given new power; as if new senses had been created fit for other worlds, and given to me because I had more to feel."

She looked at Oldys and then again at the stricken man — struck down in his youth and strength and comeliness — a

comeliness, a consummate physical fair-
ness that hardly seemed native to our
cramped times, but rather something freshly, freely, grandly pagan.

"Before," she continued, "I should have
been unworthy even to mourn him, for to
mourn rightly we must know what we have
lost, and now—"

"Annette," said Oldys, "such raving is
senseless."

"I loved him — I loved him," she repeated with increasing vehemence, "and
he loved me. Sometimes I almost doubted
if it could be so, but he loved me. He
saw me, beautiful as he was, and did not
find me ugly; with all his goodness and
nobility he did not think me despicable.
He found me worthy of his love and I am
satisfied. He may die, but he shall live in
my heart, my thoughts; and while reason is
left to me not even a remorseless God can
take him from me. I—"

"Annette," said Oldys, at last interrupt-
ing with a tone of some firmness the wild
onrush of her undirected exclamations,
"you must calm yourself. You will lose
your mind or make me lose mine."

The girl looked up quickly.

"Do you not hear something?" she said, sharply.

Oldys rose, and going to the window drew aside the curtain and looked out; but, after standing an instant in rigid attention, he shook his head and turned slowly away from the light.

"I do," she insisted, holding up her hand. "I can hear wheels."

She was not mistaken. Turning again in anxious expectation, Oldys almost immediately caught the rattle of wheels on the hard road, and soon the quick hoof-beats of a horse almost at full gallop.

"Go! Go!" commanded the girl. "Bring him here."

As Oldys emerged from the house he saw a horse black with sweat, spotted with foam, and a high-swung cart in which were seated two men, start out from behind the clump of trees that concealed the lodge and advance rapidly up the avenue. As the driver drew up before the steps with a strong, sudden pull that nearly threw the powerful animal on his haunches, a man stood up, who,

even before the vehicle had come to a perfect stand-still, had picked up a small leather
bag and sprung nimbly over the wheel.

"Thank God, Doctor, that you are here,"
said Oldys, seizing the new-comer by the
hand.

"An accident, sir?" asked the physician
in quick, nervous tones, as Oldys hurried
him into the house.

"My son-in-law, Mr. Daryl, was thrown
from his horse an hour ago," answered
Oldys. "He has been unconscious ever
since."

"It is serious, then," and the doctor spoke
with an intonation that plainly showed that
he had expected to find only some trifling
injury that apprehension had magnified.

"Serious!" repeated Oldys, almost
shocked. "It is death."

He had tried rigorously to maintain his
composure, but with the last word his voice
broke.

"Doctor," he continued, as they hastened through the hall, "you may have two
lives dependent upon you. It would kill
her—my daughter."

"I understand," said the physician, bowing his head gravely. "It was their honeymoon."

"They were married only three months ago."

They had reached the door of the room in which the injured man lay.

"She is with him now," said Oldys, softly. "She has not left him."

The doctor nodded shortly. ·

He was scarcely a significant, though certainly not an insignificant looking man. Young, hardly yet with foot upon the plateau of middle age, he was still slightly bald and decidedly inclined to stoutness. His face, though common in type, was intelligent in expression, and the quickness of his motions suggested a certain quickness of mind. A poor country practitioner, he was evidently somewhat awed by his surroundings, and this sudden call to a new scene and unusual responsibilities had clearly disturbed him.

"I have telegraphed to town," said Oldys, as they paused before the door, "to Doctor Tisdale, to come on a special train if necessary."

The young physician bowed with a quick
expression of disappointment. It was clear
that he was half fearful of undertaking the
duties so unexpectedly placed upon him,
but it was equally evident that he desired
that this chance of distinguishing himself
should not be lost.

"We will hope," he said, "that we shall
not need his aid."

Annette glanced up as the two men entered the room.

"Doctor Stilphin," said Oldys, in the low
tone in which he had before spoken to his
daughter.

Annette looked questioningly at the man
upon whom so much—so much that seemed
absolutely vital to her—depended. That his
appearance did not wholly satisfy her was
evident, for a quick look, that would perhaps have been simply one of impatience
under ordinary circumstances, but which
the excitement of the moment raised to an
intensity almost expressing dislike, swept
across her face.

Stilphin stepped to the window and drew
back one of the curtains, the excluded light

12

rioted in with unchecked license. As it happened, the clear, strong rays fell upon the bed, revealing Daryl's perfect head and body. The power of his beauty had always been remarkable, for it was of that attractive, appealing character in which there is still no loss of manly characteristics, and its effect upon Stilphin was now evident and instantaneous. He looked at the man lying before him with sympathetic attention and quickened interest.

Suddenly, as if the light had some reviving power, the indescribable evidence of a struggling and returning consciousness appeared in the face. Though there was no absolute return of color, there seemed to come a mysterious, indeterminate change of hue over the pallid skin. Daryl raised his hand weakly, unsteadily, to his head, and breathed more easily and naturally; then he slowly opened his eyes. With a quick cry Annette sprang to her feet and bent over him. Daryl seemed to recognize her and smiled faintly—only with a quick loosening of the lips, but still with something of the sweetness of expression that so easily won men's favor and women's hearts.

"You are not dead," she almost whispered in wonder and in awe.

The smile, if it could be called a smile, appeared again ; quick and fleeting as before, but now a little more clearly marked. Still he did not speak.

"If you will let me see," said Stilphin, gently.

Annette stepped slowly away.

Bending down, the doctor, with the deftness of skill and the despatch of experience, commenced the usual medical examination. Feeling here, listening there, and all the time watching the dull, staring eyes in the white face, he went on with his work, the girl following his every motion in agonized expectation, in unrelieved apprehension.

The doctor's ear, close to the mouth of the injured man, caught a low, sibilant sound. It was so slight that no one but he, placed as he was, could hear it. With the instinctive discretion that makes a physician a diplomat, he did not appear to notice it; still, in quick recognition of the fact that Daryl wished to speak to him he nodded his head quickly. He felt, rather than saw, that the struggling lips again moved. He bent lower. In his position Stilphin could hear the sound of the slightest respiration, the least articulation; listening eagerly, he first distinguished a syllable, then a word, finally a broken sentence.

"A mo—a moment—alone," whispered Daryl, in what might have seemed only a long-drawn breathing.

"Mrs. Daryl," said Stilphin, with an air of greater confidence than he had hitherto shown, "you need rest. You had better leave us."

"I have not left him," she answered, firmly. "I will not leave him now."

"Annette," remonstrated Oldys.

"Let me stay with him while he lives," she continued, her voice changing from a tone of disdainful decision to one of abject supplication. "He may die in the next moment—he may be dying now. Let me stay and—"

Daryl turned his head in her direction, took her right hand in his and raised it to his lips, then let it fall with a look that was almost a dismissal and a farewell.

The girl turned slowly away, tears filling her eyes for the first time.

" You too had best go," said Stilphin to Oldys. " You are most needed by your daughter."

Oldys did not hesitate, his real interest was with his child. He stepped beside Annette, as she cast one quick, backward look at Daryl to see if he might not yet recall her banishment, and together they left the room. As the door closed Stilphin resumed his former attitude, leaning anxiously over the still motionless man. Almost as if breaking away from some restraining physical grasp, Daryl seemed to free his intelligence from its obscurity.

"I have been hurt," he said, in a voice grown stronger, but still weak and husky. " Shall I live ?"

" I do not know," answered Stilphin after an instant's hesitation.

"You can tell me," said Daryl, calmly. " I can bear it."

The doctor did not answer.

" Then I am dying," continued Daryl, now in almost his habitual tone. " I felt it

with my first consciousness, and wished to
speak to you alone."

Stilphin bowed.

" I am in great pain," Daryl went on, " I
can hardly breathe, but there is something
I must do or have done before I die. You
can do more for me in aiding me in this
than in helping me to a few more hours of
life."

" My professional duty—"

" A physician's duty is to his patient,
not to himself," interrupted Daryl, impatiently.   " I tell you that you can help
me in other ways more than you can with
bandages or medicines."

Stilphin stood irresolute.

" There is little time left to me," Daryl
went on. A new quality had come into
his voice; that strange, vibrant ring that
commands attention and obedience; that
stress that, heard in battle, can rally a reg-
iment or hold a forlorn hope to its purpose; that intonation that, wherever men
are gathered, impresses and sways more
than rounded phrase or incontrovertible
logic; that inflection that, coming in a love-

story, surely wins its way. "Will you do what I wish?"

"Yes," answered Stilphin. He was young inexperienced, obscure, and it was difficult for him to assert himself even in his professional capacity.

"I may die at any minute," continued Daryl; "no one else can do for me what I must have done. I must trust you."

Daryl hesitated for a moment, looking up almost beseechingly now at the doubtful man before him.

"I only ask you to write a few lines," he said. "See that they are sent to the address that I will give you, and keep all that is done — all that is written — as secret as you would, if you had it, the knowledge of your own damnation."

The doctor did not move or speak.

"A physician is like a priest," said Daryl, "what is told to him, what he learns, is guarded as closely as anything heard in the confessional."

"Yes."

"Go to the table," commanded Daryl. "There are paper and pen and ink. Write as I tell you."

Obediently as if under hypnotic influence Stilphin walked to the writing-table and seated himself before it.

The silence was for a moment unbroken by the speech of either man ; a bee that had strayed in from the gardens and that now buzzed drowsily along an upper window-pane made the only sound that could be heard in the room.

" Isabel."

Daryl's voice, coming hesitatingly, faintly, seemed to linger and then be lost in the stillness.   Stilphin looked up, amazed, fearful, doubtful as to what he should do.

" Write," commanded Daryl.

Stilphin bent over the paper and hastily traced the name he had hardly heard.

" I am dying," continued Daryl, in hurried but resolute tone, the tone of one who has much to do and but little time in which to do it.   " I have been unconscious for hours.   My first thought when I again awoke to the world was of you, as my first thought will be of you when I awake— if there is awaking — in another."   He hesitated an instant, and then went on in a

voice now weaker, now stronger, now duller,
now clearer, now harshly mocking, now
despairing, but always steadfast, relentless,
inflexible. "I am dying, and I leave you
my curse and my blessing, my hatred and
my love. I have loved you; I did not think
ever to say it, but I love you now. I
have always returned to you, and now it is
for the last time. You know how long I
have kept to my oath; you have not even
heard from me since my engagement to
Annette Oldys. What led to that engagement you do not know. I made that marriage only that I might remain near you.
Nothing could have been more shamefully
dishonorable. I knew it; still, I did not
hesitate. I had a name the world respected.
I was thought rich; I was well-looking — I
easily won the friendship of men, the love
of women. But no one knew the truth—
not even you. In a few years I became
—what? A gambler—not for the natural
excitement of play, but from the mere
desire to gain — a liar, a cheat, a scoundrel. Finally all was gone. I might be dis-
graced. I loved you. I was hard-pressed,

threatened, in danger. I knew that poverty even more than disgrace would remove me from you. I became engaged to Annette Oldys. I was ruined and she was rich. As one thinking only of gain I had approached her, seeking only her money—money that would enable me to hold my position in my world and remain near you. I at first thought of her with indifference, almost with pity. I had seen her a quiet, shy girl, moving through life half fearful of herself and others, timid and abashed by the consciousness of her immense wealth. I did not know her then; soon, however, I began to understand what—how much — she really is. I learned that she loved me; learned how such a one as she could love; learned for the first time what love really is. I say she loved me; she loved rather the being she thought I was, as she now loves the being she thinks I am—for to her the vision and the being are one. It may be through the kindness of an all-foreseeing God that I am to die. My death will pain her for a time, but what she thinks me to be will always live in her very heart and soul, and

she will be happy with that memory. If
I—the I that I am—had lived you know
what would have happened. I have not
seen you for months; what little of honor
there was left in me seemed, in her presence, to return to me and bid me forget
you—but I must have seen you soon. For
months I have been strong, fighting with
myself as I thought I had not the power
to fight for anything right; but during the
last few days I have felt the old weakness
of purpose that always brought me back
to you. If I had lived I could not have
helped it. I should have gone back to
you — you would have given me double
welcome, because my return would have
brought you two victims instead of one.
Annette would have known the truth about
me, and then she would really have lost me.
As it is, I shall die and she will never know,
and will be happy in that ignorance."

Daryl had hesitated frequently in his dic-
tation, waiting for strength to go on; now
he drew his hand feebly across his eyes and
the pause was long.

"I send this letter to the old address,"

he continued at length and even more hastily, as if fearful that his strength would not
permit him to finish. "I hope it will reach
you. I am too weak to write; another has
written for me." He stopped and asked
abruptly, "What is your name?"

"Stilphin," said the doctor.

"If you receive this letter," continued
Daryl, "and if, after a year, you have heard
nothing further, send a thousand dollars—
five thousand—what you will, to Doctor
Stilphin, at Barborough, in this State. You
will see that this is done—so much you
can do for me."

Again Daryl paused.

"I could not die without letting you
know what I have done, what I have suffered — for you. I do not expect that you
will love me the more for it or remember
me the longer, but the knowledge that I
now give you of my torture is my supremest
homage — my final tribute. I know best
what will please you, and I lay my agony
at your feet that you may exult in its memory. I shall die. It will be for the best.
I shall die. You will forget me; Annette

will remember me; and I — if thought is possible—shall think of you as I have always thought of you, shall forget her as I have always forgotten her."

His voice had greatly weakened, was almost gone, and he fell back heavily.

"Seal it," he murmured. "Address it—" and his voice was so low that the doctor bent over him to catch his words. Then again he seemed for a moment to rally and went on, "Bring it here — under my pillow—and when I am dead—"

As he uttered the last words all semblance of life was lost. Stilphin sprang to the bed and again bent over him.

Although the shadows are pointing their fingers towards the east — beckoning, it might almost seem, to the night — the heat is as great, the silence as absolute, as at noon. The mass of sunlight on the floor, however, is slightly yellower, and a single bird with some sense of the approach of evening has ventured from the drowsy grove and now twitters near the open window. To Oldys and Annette in the hall beyond

the closed door behind which Daryl lies,
the time, short though it has been, has
seemed endless.   Now and again they have
looked at each other with anxious eyes;
now and again they have moved in sloth-
like action; silent—in expectation so intense as to make them appear almost stolid.

At last the door opens and Stilphin appears upon the threshold.

" Is—is he dead?" asked Annette, almost
creeping forward from the place where she
had knelt beside her father, and speaking
as she might in the presence of some one
asleep.

" No," said the doctor, slowly.   " He is
not dead.   He will not die.   He will
live."

By one of those seemingly causeless
actions of the mind, the words that Felix
Oldys had read that morning, haltingly
returned to him.   " Know then that there
are tragedies greater than those that end
in death. . . . Man is given here but little
time to live and in that time works much
evil.   Is not this rather the grievous thing,

that life should continue, and that the harm, as is the nature of harm, should be without end? Tragedy lies more often in the continuance of life than in its surcease. Therefore, I enjoin you, call not a man's death a tragedy, for, if he had lived, you know not what evil might have been wrought."

A FLIRT

A FLIRT

I

" How old are you?"

" Mrs. Tom" Wychbold took a small sip
of the tea that steamed in the Capo di
Monte cup, whereon was depicted Danaë
and the Shower of Gold—one of a set
that was her last extravagance and her
latest pride—then glanced carelessly at the
person to whom the question was addressed.

" Twenty-two."

Dinah Haye, biting off a piece of bread-
and-butter, met her gaze squarely.

" And when did you come out?"

" When I was seventeen."

" Then it is five years since you were a
'bud'?"

" Yes."

" How many men have proposed to you?"

"I should say ten or a dozen—that is out and out, you know."

"Say a dozen?"

"Oh, yes, you may safely say a dozen."

"How many times have you been engaged?"

"Three times."

"The first?"

"When I was seventeen."

"Before you came out?"

"Yes."

"The next?"

"When I was nineteen, and again when I was twenty."

"Why was the first broken?"

"Because I was a perfect baby and didn't know any more than to get into it."

"And the second?"

"Because he was very nice and I was horribly bored in the country, and—well, when I got to town I thought better of it."

"And the third?"

"Because he was very rich and every woman tried to marry him; but when I found I could, I really didn't want to do it."

"Dinah, you're a flirt."

"I know it."

"Dinah," said Mrs. Wychbold, as severely as it was possible for her ever to say anything, "you are really a very shocking person."

"I am not sure about that."

"At least you acknowledge that you are a coquette."

"Yes."

The animated and somewhat pointed dialogue here recorded took place in Mrs. Wychbold's pet withdrawing-room, where, at five o'clock, the arcana of afternoon-tea always awaited the initiate, and where "Mrs. Tom" and Dinah Haye—her guest—the only votaries at that solemn ceremonial on this occasion present, were seated. The light had nearly disappeared from the dull January sky, and the room had become quite dark — so dark that even the small lamp burning under the kettle of hot water cast an orange glow on the little table that bore the tea-things. No sound but the gentle purr of the escaping steam and the genial crackle of the blazing wood broke the silence for a moment, and then Mrs. Wychbold spoke again.

" Dinah," she asked, remonstrantly, " why will you do this ?"

" Do what ?"

" Flirt."

" Why shouldn't I ?"

" I know," conceded " Mrs. Tom," " that I shouldn't think, on general principles, any more of a girl who wouldn't flirt—a little, on occasion—than I should of a man who wouldn't fight."

" Well then ?" Miss Haye observed.

" But you don't do it a little, you do it a great deal—all the time—invariably."

" Suppose I do ?"

" There's sure to be trouble—if not for others, then serious harm to yourself — if you keep on."

" I don't know about that," answered Dinah, stubbornly.

" It is sure to be so," urged " Mrs. Tom." " I suppose," she added, " that you intend to marry some day."

" I have," answered Miss Haye, " every intention of entering upon the holy state of matrimony—indeed, I am going to take particular care that I do."

"THE ROOM HAD BECOME QUITE DARK."

" But," said Mrs. Wychbold, triumphant-
ly, "what man do you think will ever care
about marrying you when you've been carrying on—throwing yourself away on the
dozens of others that you have?"

" Dozens ?" responded Dinah, critically;
"that's liberal, even lavish; but I pass it
by, knowing as I do the usual luxuriance
of your descriptions. I maintain, however,
that many a man of sense will be very glad
to marry me in spite of all that— perhaps
even because of all that."

"Merciful heavens !" cried Mrs. Wychbold, dismayed by such ample confidence
and such utter degeneracy, "what do you
mean ?"

" I mean, my dear Constance," said Miss
Haye, calmly, "that I have come, through
time and experience, to know something
about the world and, what is more, the
men who live in it, and I assure you that
any one who succeeds in winning my smiles
—I believe that is quite the sanctified
phrase—will do something of which he may
be proud. I mean that I have discrimi-
nation, powers of comparison —have, in

short, a standard, which no girl who has not gone through what I have, can possibly possess. Now, I tell you, men of sense have sense enough to realize this—that is, *nice* men, men who are 'worth while'—and they therefore find me more attractive, more satisfactory, than the pretty, petty little prude who came out yesterday, and who would receive another, to whom they would hardly take the trouble to nod in their club, as well as she would them. Don't you suppose that they want their worth recognized? I'm an expert, and my approbation means appraisal at their own valuation. That's the reason that they would rather have me care for them than any mere 'bud' or guarded hot-house blossom who will fall in love with the first idiot who comes along."

" And you think that men like a flirt ?"

" I think they—that is, those who are worth anything—like women who can understand and appreciate them, and *that*, I am sure, few of your rigidly reserved and rigorously respected damsels, who have never talked unchaperoned to any man ex-

cept their own brothers, can ever do."
She spoke with a certain fiery vigor, and
then breaking for a moment into low laughter at her own earnestness, she added,
"Besides, the day of the ''aughty Imo-
gene' has gone by."

"What do you mean?" asked Mrs.
Wychbold.

"I mean that nowadays men don't want
to think of women as if they were enshrined
saints or pedestalled goddesses. I don't
know whether we or they have changed,
or whether it is that we as a race have
lived in the world so long that we don't
feel such strangers to one another. I don't
know what a *parfait knight* ' or a *preux
chevalier*' may have felt, but I know that
any man of this, of our generation, would
vote a woman a bore who, after years of
devotion, would only drop him a flower
from some lofty battlement or, after seasons of attention, would only concede to
him the right to kiss the pink nail on her
little finger; he would ride or walk away
with a shrug of his shoulders and have
nothing more to do with her. Our men

may have been spoiled—I don't know; but we've got to take them as we find them, or not take them at all."

"Dinah," said Mrs. Wychbold, "you shock me very much."

"I know," Dinah went on with some bitterness, "there are a great many old ladies who don't think me 'nice'; a number of very sweetly inoffensive girls who don't consider me 'proper'; some very worthy mothers of families who would be glad to call me 'not respectable,' but I cannot help it, for I cannot help my education or my age. I—" and again she laughed her soft, sweet, indulgent laugh, "I am a *product*."

"I am glad, Dinah," said Mrs. Wychbold, "to know so accurately what you are. I was always a little doubtful."

"I never could have existed at any other time," went on Miss Haye; "there wasn't any place for me. I should have scandalized your mother and horrified your grandmother, while you—you love me, don't you, Constance, dear?"

"Yes," answered "Mrs. Tom," reluctantly. "I'm afraid that I do."

"That's because we're of the same day
—speak the same language, or rather the
same dialect, and are influenced by nearly
the same motives, *modistes*, and men—for,
my dear 'Mrs. Tom,'" said Dinah, with suddenly assumed formality, "you know that
they say you are 'fast' too."

"I know it," admitted Mrs. Wychbold,
"although I could never understand why."

"What chance would there be for me if
I were not what I am?" continued Miss
Haye with greater seriousness. "Every
one has to be pronounced to-day to be
prominent; one must be characteristic, even
if one hasn't character — and I am only
a little more pronounced, more characteristic, than another—have all the 'points'
of my class, so to speak. You—they—
may think the class deplorable, but I'm
really not so much to blame if I do belong
to it. I always had to fight my own bat-
tles. I never have had chances but those
I made myself, and if people think that
an American girl with the blood of a self-
made American father in her veins and
the spirit of a nervous American mother

in her heart is not going to be ambitious,
isn't going to try and 'get on,' they shut
their eyes on all the teachings of science
and absolutely disregard the great doctrine
of heredity. Oh, if I were Cynthia Leigh,
for example, with her pale, pretty eyes, her
dull yellow hair, her pink-and-white com-
plexion, and her many, many millions, I
don't know but what I might have been
as ignorant, as helpless, as—as 'respected'
as she; but I have had to trust to the attractiveness of my own brown eyes—you
know you always said that I had 'honest
eyes'—and so, naturally, I have made the
most of my few advantages. I may have
'pushed' and I may have 'struggled'—
strange that what is considered a merit in
an American man is something for condem-
nation in an American girl—but I will tell
you one thing, Constance Wychbold, and
that is that I never have had a bit of a
flirtation—I hate the word as much as any
one—when I didn't put some of my heart
in it, mistakenly though it may have been.
And I will tell you another thing, and that
is that a girl never can know anything

about a man if she doesn't flirt with him."

"But," asked Mrs. Wychbold, "is it dignified, is it self-respecting?"

"Dignified?" cried Miss Haye, her fresh, strong, young voice becoming in tone still more elevated. "With their 'dignity' and 'self-respect' women have managed to lose the position they ought really to hold. Nature never intended that things should be managed the way they are. Why, Constance, I was reading in a book the other day that the reason why masculinity among the birds of the air, the beasts of the field, and the fishes of the sea gets itself up so 'regardless' is simply to find favor with the dear, darling femininities of their own kind. Now, how is it with us? Are not we the ones to array ourselves in the most gorgeous habiliments merely that we may gratify and attract our fellow-men? Is this right? Are not the purposes of an all-wise and provident nature clearly perverted? And how has this happened? It has happened because woman has tacitly yielded up her right of 'selection,' and merely

taken her place in the ranks of those to
be chosen from." Miss Haye paused to
laugh at her own eagerness. 'You blame
me, and yet you see I refer to nature. I
do more consciously, and perhaps more
conscientiously, what all my little sisters
are doing more or less blindly; for, after
all, every sensible person knows that women
make love just as much as men—only perhaps in another way."

" Oh, Dinah !" remonstrated " Mrs.
Tom."

" You cannot deny," continued Miss
Haye, " that you let Tom Wychbold know
that you thought he was charming long before he offered you his heart and hand."

" Yes, I know," interrupted " Mrs. Tom,"
" but I never made love to him."

" La Rochefoucauld omitted to remark,"
said Miss Haye, sententiously, " that the
woman who permits a man to make love
to her is after her own fashion making
love to him."

Mrs. Wychbold carefully deposited her
cup on the table, and then sank back in
her chair softly laughing.

" Dinah," she said, " I never saw you excited. Why, you are actually angry."

" It is the accumulated indignation of years," answered Miss Haye, speaking again with her low, sweet, mocking drawl. " But didn't you say something about the cards for the dinner-table ?"

" Yes," answered Mrs. Wychbold, " won't you write them ? I'm so frozen that I'm going to hug the fire. I could envy the fate of a martyr at the stake."

Miss Haye sat down before " Mrs. Tom's " inlaid unbusiness-like desk with a very business-like air.

" Who's coming ?" she demanded, with doubtful English, but purposeful energy.

" Ruth Redmond and Harold," said Mrs. Wychbold.

" Yes," said Dinah as she wrote.

" Frank Nesbitt."

" I do dislike him," commented Miss Haye.

" I am sorry my guest isn't happy in pleasing you," responded " Mrs. Tom "; " but between ourselves I don't like him very much myself."

"I don't care for that instructive kind of man," said Dinah, "and then he does fancy himself such a lot."

"But you know he is very intellectual, and Cynthia and he will get on capitally."

"Poor lamb," said Miss Haye; "she'll drink of the troubled waters of his eloquence and think it is a divine draught."

"She's old enough to look out for herself."

"Yes, she's old enough," answered Miss Haye, "but she's exactly the kind I've been talking about: she doesn't know herself or anybody else. She's just the sort that some wolf will gobble up, millions and all—or millions and nothing."

"I hope you'll get on together," said "Mrs. Tom," anxiously.

"Oh," responded Miss Haye, "she'll think I'm 'horrid' and 'unladylike' and all the rest; but I don't believe we'll quite tear each other's eyes out. You know that I couldn't afford to run the risk of losing mine."

"She comes on the five-thirty train," said Mrs. Wychbold, glancing at the clock.

"I hope she'll be in time for dinner at half-past seven."

"Next," added Miss Haye, and she again disposed herself for further calligraphic efforts.

"Milnes Desborough," said Mrs. Wychbold.

As Dinah wrote this name on the small bit of card-board before her she bent her head very low over the table. Certainly the night had shut in suddenly and the room was really dark.

"I observe," said "Mrs. Tom," critically, "that you do not say anything."

"Why," exclaimed Dinah, looking up with an air of innocent unconsciousness that would have utterly deceived a less experienced person than her hostess; "is there anything to say?"

"No, not in the least," responded Mrs. Wychbold, "certainly not. Only, Dinah, I have met people, and I am convinced you are one of them, the extent of whose thoughts you cannot surely measure by the abundance of their expression."

Miss Haye collected the cards, which she

14

had placed in a row before her, into a small pack and shuffled them thoughtfully.

"I understand your insinuations, Constance," she said, "and scorn them. But then, you know, what can you expect? I'm only a flirt."

"I would tell you to be careful only Milnes Desborough is old and experienced enough in all conscience to look out for himself, and, moreover, too busy a person to think of such a trifling creature as yourself. There are some men who the world seems to decide off-hand will get on, and he is one of them. His fate is to marry money and to become a public character. I feel it just as much as does the rest of the world."

"Now tell me all the others," commanded Dinah, briefly.

Miss Haye rose a trifle languidly when all the cards were written; then, returning to the fire and leaning her head against the carved mantel, she looked curiously at the blaze.

"I suppose Cynthia would be just the sort of inoffensive person such a man would

admire; he'd think her so womanly, and
I, you know — I'm only womanish, and
that's so different."

Dinah hesitated.

"And she's so rich," she went on.

"It would be a very proper match in every
way," answered Mrs. Wychbold, decidedly.

Miss Haye drew her foot slowly along
the line of the hearth and then turned
quickly towards the door.

"I must go and dress," she said, "and
so, Constance, must you."

II

In one of the bow-windows of the Andros Club were seated two men; the dusk
of the closing day permitting the dull fire
at the end of the cigarette of the one and
the cigar of the other to glow redly and
distinctly.

"Who, Harold," asked the older and
heavier of the two, knocking the ashes
from his cigar, "is this Miss Dinah Haye?"

Redmond laughed.

"Why, Milnes," he said, "you don't say
she's here?"

"Yes," answered Desborough, "at 'Mrs. Tom's.'"

"Well," said his companion, "she's a young person who has flirted her way over two continents and through five seasons, and who—"

"I don't mean that, but—who is she—where does she come from—to whom does she belong?"

"She's the daughter of a man, dead now, who in his time was one of the most prominent lawyers of Arapago. Lived well and died poor. You know the kind—a little politics and a large house, a turn for speculation and a fancy for horseflesh. Dinah, when she was a small child, romped through the parlors of every watering-place hotel in the country with the dress of a little millionnairess; but when her father dropped off there wasn't even money enough to keep her at the swell school where she then was. However, things looked up a bit afterwards; the widow moved into a small house, gathered up the odds and ends, and there's been sufficient to send the boy to college and keep Miss Dinah scampering over the old world and the new since she was seventeen."

" But—" began Desborough.

" She's an institution," continued Redmond, warming up to his subject. " Why, at Homburg, when I was there two seasons ago, she was the rage. They called her 'Roulette,' because, they said, 'you never knew where she'd stop'; but I—as a compatriot—who'd seen her like before, understood that she knew very well where to stop and what she was about. I'm not sure but I was rather in love with her myself, although we'd been together a summer at Narragansett when her dresses only came to the top of her shoes and she was the wildest little piece that ever looked like a Yankee Greuze and talked as nearly as she knew how like an American Gavroche. To me even, who'd been brought up with that kind all my life, she was a revelation, and a certain royal personage said that although he thought it was no longer in the power of America to surprise him, she had done it."

" Then," said Desborough, "I have been

entertaining an angel unawares, for I sat
out three dances with her last night and
didn't realize her peculiar greatness."

"Three dances out! That's more than I
ever saw her give the heaviest guardsman."

"Really!" responded Desborough, with
a visibly satisfied laugh; "you see I'm not
quite a pensioner on the good-humor of
the gay world."

"But take care," went on Redmond.
"You must know she's the most dangerous little flirt that ever stood on heels
two inches high."

"I don't think," answered his friend,
"that you need have any particular fear
about me. You know I'm old-fogy and
old-fashioned, and she's not my style at
all. It was pleasant enough talking to
Miss Dinah while it lasted, but—Heaven
defend me from a lifetime of it."

"I always liked the little girl," said Redmond, reflectively, "and have never seen
any harm, but rather a lot of good in her,
even if she is the terror of all chaperons
with prim and proper charges, and of all
doting mammas with utterly hopeless hope-

fuls. They'd rather see the Fiend himself
in a ball-room than Dinah Haye, though
why I'm sure I can't understand, as she
would no more think of robbing a wall-
flower of her occasional prey than she
would of stealing her stray cotillon favor."

"I think," said Desborough, "I understand her perfectly—the type of girl that
men consider 'good fun,' but would never
dream of marrying."

"Stuff and nonsense!" ejaculated Redmond. "There are enough who would have
liked and would like to marry her."

"You'll find men who will cross the
Atlantic in a small boat," answered Desborough, "but the most still prefer the se-
curity of the conventional Cunarder." Then
he continued, with a yawn, "But, as matrimony's not my lay, I think I may go on
without any fear of burning my fingers, and
learn a little more about this manifestation
of nineteenth-century femininity."

"Milnes," answered Redmond, "I suppose that you've all the principles and
prejudices that rightly belong to the scion

of so distinguished a New England family
—are thoroughly imbued with all the puri-
tanics, if you'll allow me the word—but as
for myself—I'm married now and can speak
my mind—I find the gentle trickle of small
talk which the average maiden of society
sees fit to inflict upon me rather thin.   No,
my dear fellow, give me the much-abused
girl of the day, who knows her own mind
and the minds of others; who can walk
along the brink of the steepest precipice
without losing her head, and who, indeed,
has coolness enough to hold out a helping
hand to you when she sees you are growing dizzy — give me the modern maiden,
'the great, the glorious, the ever-free,' such
as she is to-day—hardly to be excelled in
the future—certainly never equalled in the
past."

"My dear Harold," said Desborough,
"you are impassioned in your style, but
really, don't you think this is a subject
that you and I should have dropped long
ago?"

"Not when you still sit out three dances,"
answered Redmond.

"That"—Desborough hesitated—"that was an exception."

"Of course it was," said his friend. "But so is Dinah an exception — an exception among a lot of exceptions—nothing quite so perfect of the kind in the country."

"But the kind?"

"Believe me, there's a great deal to say for the kind. Why, man, she and the great many like her, that we have around us, are only another instance of ' demand and supply.' "

"What do you mean?" asked Desborough.

"Mean?" said Redmond. "I mean that we ask a great deal more of our girls than did our daddies. We demand that they shall meet us as human beings, with equal knowledge, equal abilities, almost equal experiences. The mute, unquestioning adoration and obedience with which our grandfathers were satisfied would bore us nearly to death ; we want a woman who can understand our hopes, our fears, our pleasures, and our pains—who, as pretty as or prettier even than her foremothers, has, besides,

intelligence, learning, wit, taste, and ten
thousand other things, the requirements of
an exacting generation. I tell you there's
a great call for fresh, strong, *militant* girlhood just now, and you are demanding it
just as much as any one else. Proof: The
fact that you sat out three dances with
Dinah Haye, which you never would have
done with one of your offish, icy damsels,
even if she would let you."

"But dances are one thing and marriage
is another," remonstrated Desborough.

"Perhaps; but think how highly absurd
for a man to marry a girl who would bore
him if he danced with her only half a doz-
en times."

"Did you ever see Cynthia Leigh?"
asked Desborough.

"Yes, often, and should have found her
charming — in another and better world.
Here, she's really about as much use as,
say, a good statue of herself."

"I have always admired her very much."

"Of course you have. So have I — so
have we all of us. It's the thing to do.
She is correct; she is traditional; she is

the highest ideal of which the past was capable; she is the '*ingénue*,' the undoubted, well-authenticated '*ingénue*'; but, Desborough "—Redmond paused a moment— "we've got, with a great many other good things, a higher ideal in these our slandered days. We do not extol and exalt the ignorance that understands nothing and consequently fears nothing; but rather, praise that bright, clear intelligence that, knowing much, knows also when and where to reflect, to hesitate, to pause, to stop."

"You might shake the faith of somebody else perhaps," said Desborough, smiling at Redmond's vehemence, "but it takes more than one or two generations to dilute the old Puritan blood, and I shall continue to believe in the 'meek and lowly maid.'"

"All right," answered Redmond, good-humoredly; "she was good in her time and her place; indeed, her virtues are not forgotten, but only included in the many merits of her modern substitute — taken for granted by this age that asks for—"

"'Militant girlhood,'" laughed Desbor-

ough, noting Redmond's pause and sup-
plying him with his own expression.

"Yes, that's it, 'militant girlhood,'" continued Redmond, quickly. "If you want
the other thing, you'll have to go back to a
past when the world didn't experience so
many sensations to the square inch and the
round minute. I don't say that it wasn't
better, but it won't do now"; then he added
laughingly,

"Oh, for old Saturn's reign of sugar-candy!—
Meantime I drink to your return in brandy."

The two men sat in silence for a moment.

"You dine at the Wychbold's?" said Desborough at length.

"Yes; don't you?"

"Yes," answered Desborough, rising.
"Then I'll see you there?"

III

The dinner had advanced several stages
—had attained that point where, if at any
time in a dinner's course, the wine and the
wit should sparkle—when Dinah turned
from her left-hand neighbor.

"I don't remember," said Desborough, "that I have lately done anything that was particularly good and noble."

"What do you mean?"

"And yet I must," he went on, "or certainly I shouldn't deserve such good-fortune."

"What good-fortune?"

"My being just here."

"I hope you are not disappointed," she said.

"Why?"

"For one reason, because you ought not to be here."

"What moral obligation," asked Desborough, who had found himself consigned to his present place with a feeling of supreme satisfaction, "what particular rule is outraged by my occupying this chair?"

"The highest law known to society," answered Dinah, "the will of your hostess."

"But," said Desborough, with some bewilderment, "I am duly billeted—I found my name at this place."

"Yes," answered Dinah, "but it's all wrong."

"What do you mean?"

"I mean," answered Dinah, smiling and rolling a crumb of bread under her finger, "that I slipped down before dinner and changed the cards. I wonder if you will forgive me?"

"For what?"

"For having taken upon myself to interfere—to act the part of a guardian angel—when I wasn't sure that you wanted one."

"I think," Desborough answered, "that you must have known that my own had given me up as a bad job, and that you wished to give me a chance. But where should I have been?" he asked. "Ah, yes, I see; my place was intended for Nesbitt."

"Of course," said Miss Haye; "but I can't bear him, and I wanted to talk to you."

"Why," said Desborough, in surprise, "I thought he was the gilded ornament that crowned this particular social edifice—the pet of both the 'débutante' and the 'dowager'—the amiable, the accomplished, the wholly admirable."

"Oh, yes, but I cannot endure his transcendental poetry or his equally transcendental politics."

Desborough had always been thought a sensible person, but he was not so exaltedly superhuman that he did not experience a slight feeling of gratification at hearing Miss Haye speak in this impulsive and decided fashion of a man whom he had in his heart always despised.

"However," she continued, "I suppose that is because I'm not intellectual."

"Perhaps," said Desborough, laughing. "Do you know I had not thought of that."

"Well," she went on, "I'm not, and don't pretend to be; but if I were, I'm sure I'd never let any one suspect it. Don't you think there is such a lot of 'pose'?"

"Yes," answered Desborough, thinking of the many weary minutes during which he had been obliged to submit to the process of having himself impressed. "I think intellect is too often the last resort of weak minds."

Miss Haye laughed gleefully.

Just as "Mrs. Tom" glanced up and

down the table with the all-enveloping look
of the hostess who is about to rise, Dinah
again turned to Desborough, with whom she
had not been talking for full five minutes.

"You are sure you are not sorry?" she
insisted.

"Perfectly," he replied.

"Because you know if you hadn't been
here you would have been somewhere else."

"Are you stating that as a physical fact,
or as a social truth?"

"As a social truth," she answered, smiling; and following her glance he saw that
it rested on Miss Leigh.

No, he certainly was not sorry; with Cynthia he knew that he should have been expected to be "on parade," and he was consciously grateful to Dinah for permitting
him the luxury of airing his thoughts, in
what at best was but a "fatigue dress."

"And you are really going already?" he
said, as, standing, he pulled away her chair.

"Yes, thank you; and I suppose that if
we are very good and patient you will join
us—at last."

IV

The Wychbold carriage—an exquisite little one-horse brougham that became " Mrs. Tom " admirably — was rapidly bowling along the smooth, hard macadam road beside the Park " meadows," where the snow lay at the roots of the long grass as the white sand lies about the flags that grow along a beach.

" Do you think he really cares for her?" asked Dinah, drawing up the fur robe over her face until only her eyes and her forehead were visible.

" I don't know," answered Mrs. Wychbold, blandly. " I'm sure he never came to the house so often before."

" But—" began Dinah, her voice dulled by the heavy folds of the voluminous covering.

" Certainly," interrupted " Mrs. Tom," " it's not to see me, and you cannot for an instant imagine it's to see you. Besides, nothing could be more natural; a man of his traditions would be sure to fancy such a girl as Cynthia. Some men are so dull

15

about some things, and mistake primness
for profundity, insensibility for dignity,
and vanity for just pride. Remember, I
shouldn't talk to any one else in this way,
for I am really very fond of her and appreciate her fully—but sometimes she does
exasperate me very much."

"And do you believe she thinks about
him?" asked Miss Haye, still from the
depths of the thick robe.

"Not a bit," said "Mrs. Tom," decidedly
and contemptuously; "she's too inexperienced—too simple-minded, if you like—to
see anything that isn't just thrust upon her
attention, and as Milnes Desborough does
not 'pose,' she doesn't notice him. There
are some women who are only attracted by
affectations, who will only bite at the artificial fly."

"And that is the reason she likes Nesbitt?"

"Exactly. She is taken by all his sil-
liness and assumption, because they seem
like something she has been taught to believe is 'intellectual' and fine and elevated
and all the rest. She thinks she is listen-

ing to words of profoundest wisdom, not
knowing that it is all extracted from the
last reviews. She cannot understand that
the men who do anything haven't much time
to talk, and that when they do, they generally say something of their own, even if it
is nonsense. I never could endure Frank
Nesbitt after I heard how he treated one
poor girl."

" What did he do ?"

" I learned it in a queer way, but I
know that the story is true. He was engaged to a very pretty young thing whom
he threw over at the end of three years,
because, as he told her, with great mag-
nanimity, he could not bear the idea of her
enduring the life of poverty that must be
theirs if they married ; for you know he
hasn't a cent, and no more had she."

" I never heard anything of it."

" He never allowed the engagement to be
announced, and so when it was broken off
there was no talk. Oh, I never could trust
him. You know none of the men like
him."

" Yes," answered Dinah.

"Cynthia must not get interested in him—she shall not," asserted "Mrs. Tom." "Marriage is a very serious thing and—I don't see why you are always going and getting into it."

"I've not," Dinah observed; "but this from you, who made a notorious love-match, and to whom all society points as the one perfect example of bliss in a brown-stone 'cottage'!"

"Dinah," said "Mrs. Tom," grasping Miss Haye's hand beneath the fur wrappings, "you don't know all."

"What is it, Constance?" asked Dinah in surprise.

"I am perfectly miserable."

"Constance," cried Miss Haye, "tell me immediately what you mean."

"I can't."

"Tell me all about it," said Dinah, gently taking "Mrs. Tom's" left hand in both of hers. "I saw that there was something that troubled you, but I didn't like to ask."

"I wouldn't tell any one else in the world but you," replied "Mrs. Tom"; "but I feel that you will understand."

" Yes, dear," said Miss Haye.

" I don't know how it could have happened, but you know that we haven't got so very much money—that is, when you consider how awful our expenses are, and though Tom has always been as liberal as possible, I couldn't get on with what he gave me. I'd used up all my own income and I began to get into debt. I couldn't stop, and now what I owe is something fearful—and Tom doesn't know anything about it."

" Constance !"

" I know it's frightful of me, I realize that perfectly. I thought I would save and pay it, but now it is so much that—I can't and I don't know what to do."

" Tell Tom."

" I can't."

" But, Constance, this is serious. The money is nothing—"

" Nothing !"

" I perhaps might arrange all that," mused Miss Haye.

"Oh, Dinah !" cried "Mrs. Tom," forgetting where she was and clutching wildly at her friend, "if only you can find some way to save me I'll think you're—"

"A horrid, fast flirt," laughed Dinah.

"The dearest, truest, best person on earth."

"Don't," said Dinah, entreatingly; "you'd never know it was I; but, suppose I do find a way, what will you do besides think me all these impossible things?"

"I'll promise you," answered "Mrs. Tom," "never, *never* to be extravagant and never to do anything like it again."

Miss Haye sat silent for a moment, gazing intently across the swelling park lands at the leafless trees, on the topmost branch of the tallest of which a crow sat cawing dismally.

"Constance," she said at length, "perhaps it's just as well that I—as you say—understand."

Milnes Desborough paced slowly up Alaska Avenue in the clear twilight that had succeeded the bright winter day.

Hearing a rapid step, detecting a short, sharp footfall, he looked quickly up and saw that Dinah Haye was before him, smiling and almost barring his way.

"You!" he exclaimed—"out at this time!"

"Oh," she cried, "I am not afraid, and the air is so exhilarating, so—so drinkable —so tippleish and intoxicating!"

Desborough turned, and without much thought of what he was doing walked beside her down the street.

"By the way," he said, "your name is Dinah Haye, is it not?"

"Yes," she answered, "Dinah! Is that a name to give a white woman?"

"I was not thinking of your first name, but your last."

"Haye," she said. "I think it is a very pretty name; not aristocratic, perhaps, but still distinguished."

They had reached the "Square" at which the avenue ended, and now paused on the curbstone.

"I don't see any use of walking further," she said, abruptly.

"But—"

"Oh, I wasn't going anywhere, and now I want to go back."

A wild idea came to him at that moment. Could it be that it was solely for the purpose of meeting him that she came out?

"You will let me go back with you?" he said. "The club is up the avenue, and I always stroll that way about this time."

"I know it," she answered briefly as they turned together.

He would have liked very much to know if what his flattered vanity had quietly whispered to him was the truth, but he could think of no method of discovery, and he walked on in indolent enjoyment of her companionship.

"I knew a young fellow once," he said, "who had your name; indeed, I believe I pulled him out of the water a year or two ago at Nahant when a cramp caught him and he was in rather a bad way. He's now at Harvard, but he writes to me from time to time—I suppose to let me know that he hasn't gone to the dogs yet."

"Oh!" she exclaimed, in her excitement placing her hand on his arm. "I always knew it was you, and I always wanted to tell you, but—just speaking about it seemed so little after what you had done that I never said anything—and you saved his life."

"Really," answered Desborough, "you put it rather too picturesquely. I only picked him out of a sea that was like glass, when there were plenty about to do it if I had not."

"But they didn't," she said, "and he always told me that you saved him—he talked very often to me about you, saying that you had always been so kind to him and had done so much for him—"

"I—" began Desborough.

"And I have always thought that I should so much like to see the man who had done so much for Phil—to talk with him and tell him my gratitude. And now that I have met him I can say nothing."

"Don't," said Desborough, impatiently, "you will make me sorry I spoke. If I had not been so luxuriously apathetic at just that moment that I could not be held responsible for anything I said, I certainly should not have done it."

"But," she continued, noticing the expression of annoyance in his face, "you know that I shall never forget."

"I hope," he said, fervently, "that you will."

She did not speak at once.

"You're going to the Fenwick ball?" she said at length.

"Yes," he answered. "And you?"

"Yes, I shall be here for that."

"Here for that!" he exclaimed in surprise; "but I thought you were going to stay a long time."

"So I have been here a 'long time,'" she replied, laughing. Then she added, "And isn't it a week and a half until then?"

"A future and a fraction," he answered, evasively.

"I shall hate to go," she said. "I love 'Mrs. Tom' and I love Andros."

"And they both have a very perceptible predilection for you," he laughed.

The Wychbold house was not many blocks from the "Square," and they were soon before its door.

"Good-night," she said, holding out her

hand; "for there is nothing at which we meet until to-morrow."

"Good-night," he said, retaining her unresisting fingers in his grasp.

"You really mustn't," she said, making, however, no effort to liberate herself, "or Mrs. Abernethy across the way may think you are taking a rather lengthy 'adieu.' She disapproves of me as it is—almost, indeed, as much as you do."

She laughed — hardly mirthfully, and caught her hand abruptly away.

"How do you know I do not approve of you?" he asked, imperturbably.

"I feel it," she answered, "and I wonder I do not hate you."

"You are very indulgent."

"I think I am—but do you know I do things on purpose to shock you? I glory in it."

"I am sorry to disappoint you," he answered, "in everything. But you don't. I'm not in the least shocked. You see you are a sort of rule unto yourself, and what in another—"

"Might be reprehensible and improper

is nothing at all when I do it—is forgotten and passed over—just because it is only I."

" You do not understand," he exclaimed.

" Yes, I understand," she responded, indignantly. "Your explanation is very satisfactory—highly so."

" But you are wrong."

"No, I am right," she went on, hotly. " You think I do things that no one else would do."

" No," he protested.

" Yes," she insisted, "and I do. I told you I took particular satisfaction in horrifying you. I am going to do it once more. I came out this afternoon on purpose to meet you."

" Did you?" he demanded, eagerly.

" I know that you think I shouldn't have done it ; and if I did, that I shouldn't have told you—should have kept it a secret as if I was ashamed of it."

" But, really, did you?" he asked, with unusual earnestness.

" Yes," she answered, and as the servant opened the door she vanished from his sight.

V

Dinner had not been a very festive affair. As it had happened, the only expected guest of the evening had given out at the last moment, and the household had dinner alone. On the whole, the evening had been rather dismal. Between Dinah and Cynthia Leigh there had arisen a distant coldness. "Tom" Wychbold was evidently depressed; and even "Mrs. Tom," who generally was only not equal to an occasion when she was superior to it, sat at the head of the table in unaccustomed thoughtfulness.

At last the ordeal was over, but, when the rest had withdrawn from the dining-room, Wychbold did not, as he ordinarily would have done, seek the seclusion of his smoking-room; instead, he hovered uneasily about the drawing-room, where Miss Leigh was trying the music, just sent her, of some new composer whose name was chiefly made of the last letters of the alphabet; where "Mrs. Tom" was writing notes, and where Miss Haye was doing nothing.

"Oh!" he exclaimed at length, with a very mechanical air of carelessness, "I wish some one would come and see the way they have framed the photograph of the four-in-hand. I can't make up my mind whether it's right or not."

He looked imploringly at Dinah, and she jumped up promptly.

"I'll come," she said. "I'm always only too ready to give an opinion."

He led the way to his particular holy of *unholies*, where the chief objects of still-life were crops, spurs, and guns, and the only occupant other than themselves was a shaggy Skye terrier that came jumping to meet them; then he closed the door carefully and mysteriously, and glanced around at his companion. "I want, Dinah," he said, "to speak to you alone for a moment."

"Yes," she answered; "you certainly made it evident enough, and that's the reason that I came."

"Of course I shouldn't speak to any one else of this; but you—for you—you know —you—"

"Yes," Dinah interrupted, "I am different. I *know*—I *understand*."

" How could you guess what I was going to say?" asked Wychbold in amazement.

"Strange, isn't it?" said Miss Haye.

Wychbold again glanced around the room.

" Dinah, I've been a fool."

" It would hardly be becoming in me not to attempt at least to look decently surprised."

" There's no doubt about it, I've made an idiot of myself," continued Wychbold.

" As there are so many ways," observed Miss Haye, critically, "in which a man can make an idiot of himself, the fact that he has doesn't carry very much information. One expects that, and the only interest lies in knowing how he has done it."

" Now, Dinah, don't be hard. I want you to help me."

" I've no doubt of it—but what have you ' been and done'? Come, tell the whole truth, if you expect any aid from me."

" It all came from our going to Lake Masaqua last summer. Constance went wild about the country. She declared that

she would have a country place, and she
would not be satisfied until I promised
to buy one, which I did."

"That seems all smooth enough so far."

"Yes," groaned Wychbold, "but it isn't
all of it. She wanted to buy on Lake Masaqua and I on Lake Samaqua. She said
that Lake Masaqua was the only possible
spot—that they would be putting railroads
and hotels at Lake Samaqua, and that it
would be horrid."

"Yes."

"Well—I went and bought on Lake
Samaqua, having confidence that it was the
best thing to do, and that it would come
out all right—and have never told her anything about it, leaving her to think that the
place is Lake Masaqua."

"And how has it come out?"

"All wrong. They're going to put up a
monster hotel at Samaqua, with a railway
running up behind it"—and Tom held out
a small country newspaper to Miss Haye.
"And here is a letter offering me double
what I paid for our place."

"That hardly seems all wrong."

"Yes, but don't you see? Constance doesn't want the money, but wants the place—and the other is sold; and it has all turned out just as she said it would, and with every one that she knows going to Lake Masaqua this summer she'll be wretched if she isn't there, and altogether I'm in a hole."

"I'll see what I can do," said Miss Haye.

"Really,"said Wychbold, delighted. "Will you, really? I know that if you try you can settle it, and you must. Dinah," he continued, effusively, "do whatever you like. I trust you implicitly, and if there is anything I can ever do for you—"

"You'll do it. Well—perhaps some day I may put you to the test," said Miss Haye, turning to go.

"Dinah," said "Mrs. Tom," looking curiously at her friend, "what is the matter with you?"

The two were sitting before the fire.

"Why," cried Miss Haye, in affected alarm, "do I show symptoms of anything dangerous?"

16

" Perhaps," answered Mrs. Wychbold, gravely.

" Do not tell me," exclaimed Miss Haye, " that it is croup, whooping-cough, or measles. Anything befitting my years I could endure, but those—never."

" Yes," answered the other, slowly, " it is something quite—quite natural, even at your age."

" You relieve me very much. What is it ?"

" Dinah," said " Mrs. Tom," slowly, " if you were any one else I should say you were in love."

Miss Haye's face became a shade warmer in tint; but as the fire had fallen in at that moment and now cast a sudden glow over the place, Mrs. Wychbold might imagine it was only the coloring given it by the quick flame.

" And why any one else ?"

" Because, really, I thought you had quite got past all that sort of thing," said " Mrs. Tom," " and that you had flirted away all the heart there was in you when you were quite a small child."

" My dear," answered Dinah, quickly and

evidently unreflectingly, "you don't display
your usual perspicacity. A woman's heart
is like a sponge: it may be squeezed dry
one week and yet be soaking the next."

"Mrs. Tom" laughed.

"And then," went on Miss Haye, eagerly,
"because it may have been full of water
any number of times, is there any reason
why it may not be overflowing with rich
wine at last."

"Dinah," said "Mrs. Tom," "you are
eloquent. Shall I consider that you are
speaking in your own defence?"

"I, oh no—why should I?" answered Dinah, a trifle sadly. "Every one knows me,
and no one would dream that I, who am
without 'fear' if not without 'reproach,'
would ever become a poor, sentimental,
maudlin creature."

"I am not sure," said "Mrs. Tom,"
sagely shaking her head.

"But bless you, Constance, who could it
be? Whom do you suspect?"

"Never mind my suspicion. All that I
ask is," and she leaned and kissed Dinah
with unwonted tenderness, "that you may

not singe your wings, that you may not break your heart at last, though it would be only justice if you did."

"Nonsense," asserted Miss Haye, stoutly. "I never broke anybody's heart, no one ever took me seriously enough. I've just now and then nicked one a little bit and that is all."

"Be careful," went on "Mrs. Tom." "I wouldn't have anything happen to you, and I hope that you may be as happy as—well, as you don't deserve, but really ought to be."

"And you do not think," asked Dinah, looking up for a moment and then letting her head sink among the laces of "Mrs. Tom's" frock, "that I am altogether hard and wicked?"

"No, dear," said "Mrs. Tom," placing her hand on Dinah's head and feeling for the instant strangely old and experienced, "no, not a bit."

A sudden sob shook Dinah's pliant figure, and the "Flirt" sank on the thick rug, weeping bitterly.

VI

Celestine, " Mrs. Tom's " maid, entering
the room where Miss Haye lay on a long,
low couch reading her letters received by
the afternoon mail, approached with the
usual Gallic air of confidential mystery, and
gave her a card.

Sitting up with surprising alacrity, Dinah
took the oblong bit of paper.

" Mr. Desborough!" she exclaimed. "Are
you sure there is no mistake ?—are you sure
it is not for Miss Leigh ?"

" There eez no meestake," announced
Celestine confidently. " He ask especially
for Miss Haye."

" Really ! said Dinah, staring with wide-
eyed astonishment at her informant. "Tell
Lupton to say that I'll be down directly."

As Dinah entered the great darkened
drawing-room, where the yellow and gold
chairs stood at such unamiable distances
from each other or were gathered in such
formal groups, Milnes Desborough rose
quickly from the remote corner in which
he had been sitting.

"Come into the library," she said, before
he had a chance to speak. "Do you mind?
I always feel in this place, when there isn't
a party on, as if I were in an upholstered
Sahara."

Without waiting for an answer, she led
the way across the hall to a room where
the colors were darker and the decorations
more peaceful; where the chairs were more
calculated for comfort and the crowded
objects seemed to induce confidence.

"You don't know how surprised and
honored I feel," she said, seating herself
near the fire and picking up a magazine to
shield her face from the heat.

Desborough turned his hat nervously in
his hands.

"Miss Haye," he said, "I have come to
see you for the reason that I want to tell
you something."

"Because I would—" she said, laughing,
and with a certain scornful emphasis on
the last word.

"Yes," he answered, looking up, "because you would understand. How did you
know?"

"Oh," she answered, "that's why people always come to see me, because I 'understand.' It's my specialty. Go on."

"You may think it is strange my telling you, but you will find that I've a good reason for it."

"Of course you wouldn't dream of telling it to any one else?" she said.

"No," he replied, looking up questioningly.

"I thought so—that again is something of which I have a monopoly. But go on."

"You must have noticed, as every one has, my evident—interest in Miss Leigh."

"Yes," said Dinah, impatiently, while her eyes suddenly shone with an angry light. "Do you want to relate to me the history of your love?"

"It is most important to me you should hear me," said Desborough, soothingly; "and though I may bore you horribly, I beg as a favor you will listen."

Dinah did not answer.

"For a moment," he said, taking a paper from his pocket, "to speak of something else, I received a letter this morning. Will

you allow me to read you a paragraph
from it ?"

Dinah nodded indifferently.

" 'Dinah, dear Dinah,' " read Desborough,
" 'the best sister a fellow ever had—' "

" It's from Phil," Dinah cried in astonishment.

" Yes," he answered.

" Give it to me," she commanded, bending forward and reaching out her hand.

" You mustn't grab," he said, holding
the loosely scrawled sheet above his head ;
then, shoving back his chair, he read on :
" 'Dinah is in Andros. I hope that you'll
see her. If it hadn't been for her and you
I don't know what would have become of
me. She's regularly brought me up in the
way I should go, and the memory of the
sacrifices that she has made for me is
going to be the thing that will make something of me in the end. I tell you I'm
going to pay her back by hard work if I
can manage it. She ought to have everything, and I'm going to see that she does.
Poor Di, it's lucky she's so pretty, for she
hasn't had as much as other girls. She's

pinched herself all these years to give me
a chance, and I wouldn't be here—here at
college—if the money to pay for it had not
come out of what she should have had for
her ball-dresses.' "

"The outrageous boy!" cried Dinah,
"telling tales out of school like that! He
ought to know better."

"I am very thankful that he has," observed Desborough, carefully folding the
letter, but watching her all the time, " and
I only wish more could know what he has
written."

"Nothing but the exaggeration of the
very young," said Dinah, contemptuously.

"Hardly," replied Desborough. "But I
only read you this so that you might know
exactly what I know."

"Thank you," answered Dinah, with the
air of one who is somewhat puzzled.

"And now let me go on with my story,"
he continued. "I have been said to be in
love with Miss Leigh."

Dinah did not speak.

"I shall not attempt to describe my
feelings," he added.

"Oh," she interrupted, "such analysis must be extremely interesting—please do not omit anything."

"Of those I shall say nothing," he went on, so intent upon his subject as to be almost unmindful of her interruption, "because I don't understand it all very well myself. Every one seemed to think it was natural that I should be in love with Miss Leigh."

"Oh, yes," murmured Dinah, softly.

"And what seems reasonable to every one, in time comes to seem more or less reasonable to one's self I suppose. I must believe that my admiration for Cynthia Leigh was sincere."

Although he paused, Dinah said nothing.

"I sought," he continued, speaking after the manner of one who, making a confession, endeavors painfully to state the case fairly—who conscientiously seeks to leave out nothing that may tell against him, " in every way to win Miss Leigh's favor."

Miss Haye studied the design in the rug as if its involved characters were those of some rare palimpsest which, if deciphered, would yield secrets of inestimable value to the human race.

"Yesterday, I asked Miss Leigh to marry me," he said, finally and abruptly.

Neither spoke for a moment.

"And I suppose you have come to tell me of your engagement," murmured Dinah, still without change of attitude.

"No, indeed," he cried, amazedly. "Did you think that the reason I am here?"

"No—what—why then?" asked Dinah, looking up in quick astonishment.

"But she refused me," said Desborough, almost laughing, "flatly, absolutely, irrevocably."

Dinah sprang to her feet with closed hands and flashing eyes.

"Then," she cried, "for what possible purpose have you—"

Before Dinah could finish the sentence the library door was thrown open, and "Mrs. Tom," hastily entering, quickly stopped as her eyes fell on Milnes Desborough.

"Oh—you here?" she said, too much absorbed and excited for more formal greeting.

"Yes, 'Mrs. Tom,'" he said, rising; "although I'm not quite sure about my presence of mind, my presence of body is unquestionable."

"Well," she went on hurriedly, "now run along like a dear boy. I've a great deal to say to Dinah, and if you want to see her she'll be at the ball to-night."

"But—" began Desborough.

"No," said "Mrs. Tom," impatiently stamping her foot; "you must go now— immediately."

"Very well," responded Desborough, making his way obediently towards the door. "I go, but—"

"Hurry!" commanded "Mrs. Tom," and, as the door closed, she continued: "How fortunate it wasn't a stranger! I had to speak to you immediately. What do you think has happened to me?"

"I don't know, I'm sure," said Miss Haye, blankly and even indifferently.

"I cannot understand it. See!" and "Mrs. Tom" held out for Miss Haye's inspection a handful of letters which the postman had just left.

" What are they ?"

" All my bills receipted. What can it mean ?"

" Oh, it's very simple," replied Miss Haye. " I hope you will forgive me. I was bold enough to take it upon myself to pay them in your name."

" Pay them — you !" exclaimed " Mrs. Tom."

" That is exactly what I did !"

" Really !" exclaimed " Mrs. Tom," fairly stunned by the information ; " but where did you get the money ?"

" I borrowed it from Tom," laughed Dinah, " and now you can pay me whenever you like. I'm not an exacting creditor. I sha'n't really press you for it unless Tom comes at me, and I don't think he'll do that."

" And he lent it to you ?"

" Of course. But then what I do doesn't count. No one expects anything of me, and so I can do everything." She spoke with a certain sadness, but quickly went on with greater brightness and animation : " Imagine Cynthia Leigh borrowing money from Tom. Oh, it makes all the difference in the world what kind of a standard you're expected to live up to, and I early made mine low on purpose. So you see, Constance, there are times in this world when it's just as well to be a little 'human' and 'horrid.'"

Miss Haye slipped through the door before "Mrs. Tom" could say anything further. In the hall she nearly ran into Tom Wychbold, who was coming from his den.

"Dinah, Dinah!" he called.

"What is it?" she asked, impatiently.

"How can I ever thank you?"

"For what?" she demanded.

"About fixing it up with Constance. Only just now she said that it was such a pity that we had that Masaqua place, as no one really was going there, and that she only wished she was out of it and had never been foolish enough to get into it."

"And thereupon—" said Dinah, severely.

"Thereupon I confessed like a man— and Constance said she was delighted, and that I was very clever to have made so

much money, and everything was serene.
Dinah, you're an angel !"

"You are the first who has ever discovered it," replied Miss Haye ; and running
up the stairs two steps at a time, she entered her room, locked the door, and throwing herself on the divan she had just quitted,
buried her face in the pillow.

VII

"Mees Eh ! Mees Eh !"

It was Celestine's voice at the door, and
Dinah, who was fully dressed for the ball,
hastened to open it at her excited call.

"Mees Eh !" exclaimed the middle-aged
but vivacious tire-woman, her black eyes
snapping with excitement.

"Merciful heavens !" cried Dinah, realizing that something unusual was the matter, or otherwise "Mrs. Tom's" maid could
hardly have so far lost the dignified de-
portment she considered proper in her position. "Celestine, what has happened?"

"Nothing, Mees Eh," answered the agitated person ; "it is what *is* to happen."

"Yes, yes !" exclaimed Dinah.

"I come to you because you understand."

"Of course—naturally," said Dinah, even in her haste speaking somewhat scornfully; "it's only to be expected. My understanding is certainly something phenomenal—superhuman."

"Mrs. Wychbold, she—what it is named —lose her head if she know."

"Well," said Dinah, impatiently.

"I just learn it from Josephine, Mees Leigh's maid. I do not know that I do right to tell—but I am uncertain—it is a great responsibility, and I come to you because you understand."

"Exactly—I know all about that—only tell me what it is."

"Miss Leigh has given orders," said Celestine, drawing nearer and finally speaking in French, in the hoarse whisper of conspiracy, but with the volubility of keen interest, "that all her trunks be packed— that Josephine be ready to accompany her to-night. She will go to the ball, but she will return. The gentleman, Mr. Nesbitt, will meet her at the small gate in the Fen-

wick garden—he will drive her here, where
Josephine and the luggage will await her,
and then—" and Celestine waved her hands
with the palms outspread in a gesture
that seemed to imply that the remotest
depth of interstellar space would be the
most likely place in which to make search
for the fugitives. " It is in order," she went
on, "that Mrs. Wychbold may not know—
that Miss Leigh may get away without question, that she is going to the ball."

Dinah sat down abruptly on the nearest
chair, staring blankly at her informant,
who beamed upon her with an air of unconscious importance and ineffable satisfaction.

" Really," said Dinah at length, with her
eyes even wider open than usual, and her
lips more than slightly parted.

" This very night—in a short time," rattled off the maid. " It is necessary to act
at once."

" Yes," said Miss Haye. " What is to be
done?"

" Yes, what?" said the delighted maid.

" Mrs. Wychbold—" began Dinah.

17

"Oh, no—she must not be told," interrupted Celestine, quickly. "There would be a storm—a tempest. It must be arranged quietly, so no one will know."

"It's like the little idiot," said Miss Haye, talking to herself in her absorption, and using English that might literally be called nervous in her agitation. "Mary's little lamb was an experienced black sheep beside Cynthia Leigh. How can a girl be such a lunatic, and with Nesbitt, too? Some one must stop her."

"What does Mees Eh think," demanded the maid, impatiently.

"I don't think, Celestine. I don't know. I must reflect," and running her fingers through her hair, utterly forgetful of the time and care spent in its arrangement, Dinah sat silent in the attitude of deep cogitation, while Celestine watched her expectantly.

VIII

It was nearly twelve o'clock, and the neighborhood of the big Fenwick house resounded with the roll of hastening carriages,

and the darkness was broken by the fire-
fly flash of coach-lamps. A long string of
broughams and other covered vehicles ex-
tended down the gravelled drive and far
along the street. Every minute added to
its length, and, accompanied by the hoarse
commands of the policemen and the loud
shouts of the drivers, the line moved on
with frequent pauses. One after another
the carriages stopped under the *porte cochère*
and their occupants alighted, permitting the
occasional watchers to catch glimpses of
the muffled figures that flitted lightly up the
steps and disappeared through the hastily
opened door.

Many were coming, but the rooms were
already full, for it was after midnight.
There was such a crush as to make motion
almost impossible, and, with difficulty
through the surge of voices, one caught
the strains of the waltz of the winter.

Desborough had just arrived and made
his way hurriedly through the gathering
throng—impatiently forgetful of all but one
thing.

" Have you seen Miss Haye?" he asked

of Redmond as he passed him in the door-
way.

"Not for half an hour; not since she first
came in."

With a vigorous imprecation on his ill-
luck, Desborough continued his search.

"Have you seen Miss Haye?" he demanded of his host, whom he found just
returning from a visit to the supper-
room.

"No," answered Fenwick, carelessly, "but
'Mrs. Tom' and Miss Leigh are over there,
and she must be somewhere about."

With a perceptible increase of ill-temper
Desborough passed on. He had done the
drawing-rooms thoroughly; next he inves-
tigated the halls, and then hunted through
the conservatories; examined the stairs,
carefully scrutinizing all the dark nooks
and corners. But the object of his quest
was nowhere to be found. He tried the
second floor, reconnoitring the corridors,
and, untiring in his search, made his way
even to the billiard-room, where he ruth-
lessly disturbed a blushing couple who had
fondly imagined themselves safe.

"Where in the name of all that is illusive can she have gone?" he muttered as he descended the main stairway.

Looking down, he saw Dinah Haye directly before him at the foot of the last flight.

"Where have you been?" he asked, with no great softness of accent or suavity of manner as he came up to her.

"Come," she exclaimed, not noticing his peremptoriness and advancing a step or two to meet him. "I must speak to you immediately."

"Here, in the conservatory," he said, shortly.

There were a number of people among the big bending leaves of the tropical plants; but the light was not so glaring as elsewhere, and the place where they sat down was quite out of ear-shot of the others.

"Oh!" she cried, as he seated himself beside her; but she did not speak at once, but only laughed a little hysterically.

"Something has happened," she went on. "I am trembling with excitement, and my heart beats—" she put her hand to her side —"how my heart does beat!"

"As you have regard for my sanity," he said, impatiently, "tell me what is the matter."

"I hardly know where to begin," she exclaimed, with blazing cheeks, "but I'll try. Just as I was dressed Celestine came to me and told me that Cynthia Leigh had planned an elopement."

"What!" cried Desborough. "Cynthia Leigh?"

"Yes, Cynthia Leigh; poor thing, she must have completely lost her reason, she's so inexperienced, you know—and with Nesbitt, too."

"The wretched little beggar," murmured Desborough. "He must have known that if they were once married old Leigh could be twisted into coming around with his millions."

"Exactly, as she knew that her father could never be brought to give his consent."

"But —" began Desborough.

"Celestine told me all about it," Dinah hurried on. "He was to meet her here — at the garden gate. She could easily step

out and no one would miss her for a long
time; then he was to drive her to the house,
they were to get Josephine and the trunks,
and then away they were to go."

" Well !"

" I didn't know what to do. If I had
told Tom, there would have been a scene,
he's so headstrong; if I had told ' Mrs.
Tom,' there would be another of another
sort, she's so impulsive. I hadn't any one
but myself, and there wasn't any time to
lose."

" And—" Desborough again began.

" Before I'd got here I'd made up my
mind," said Dinah, with her breath still
coming in quick, short gasps. " In a way,
it was none of my business; but really I
couldn't stand by and see the girl make
such an utter idiot of herself; get commit-
ted to that man forever. If she wanted to
do it, I thought, let her do it calmly and on
reflection, not because she is carried away
by the romantic nonsense of it all."

" So—" said Desborough.

" So," answered Miss Haye, half laughing
and half crying, "after I had come down

with them all I just ran upstairs again, put on Cynthia's wrap, slipped out the back way—"

"Really," said Desborough, beginning to laugh.

"Yes, and met Nesbitt at the gate, in the place of Cynthia. It's only three blocks to the house, you know, and I kept the hood pulled over my face and said nothing, let him do all the talking, and he never suspected. When we got to the side door at the Wychbolds' I was out like a flash, up the steps in a second, and into the house—"

"And then?" asked Desborough, motionless in his attention.

"Then," said Miss Haye, finally giving way to laughter and letting herself go in one uncontrollable burst of wild merriment, "I left him where he was, sent for James, who had not taken out the horses, to drive me back, and here I am. I suppose he is still sitting in the hack in the dark, wondering what has become of his inamorata, and why she does not come to join him with her maid and her luggage."

Desborough fell back in his chair, laughing as he never laughed before.

"And it's a fearfully cold night," he said, when at length he could speak.

"Fearfully," assented Dinah, laughing too, but with a suggestion of something in her tone or manner that indicated that tears were not yet beyond easy call.

"You really have saved the girl from making a terrible mistake," said Desborough at length, quite seriously. "She should be deeply thankful to you."

"Perhaps," said Dinah. "Still, I don't think she would be now, even if she may be some day. How she'd hate me!"

"She'll probably never know what happened," he answered.

Both were silent for a moment.

"I have been looking for you everywhere," he broke out at length.

"You wanted to see me?"

"Wanted to see you—yes," he answered, "and now I've found you at last, you must listen to me. I have not such a tale of adventure to tell as you, but still I've got something rather exceptional to say — important to me at least. I tried hard enough to say what there was to say — this after-noon—but—"

"But," said Dinah, hurriedly, "you told me everything then, didn't you?"

"Told you everything!" exclaimed Des-borough; "why, I was just beginning when 'Mrs. Tom' interrupted."

"What more was there?" asked Dinah in unaffected surprise.

"Why in the world do you suppose I told you what I did?" he demanded, almost equally astonished.

"I am sure I could not imagine," she answered decidedly.

"Because," he said, lowering his voice and drawing a trifle nearer to her, "I did not want you to misunderstand, because I did not want to approach you under any false pretences, because — Dinah dear —I have loved you from the very first, though perhaps I did not realize it, and I wanted to know if you would be willing to marry the man whom Cynthia Leigh refused."

"And you did not love her?" she asked,

"BOTH WERE SILENT FOR A MOMENT"

looking swiftly at him and then casting
down her eyes.

"Not a bit," he answered with full con-
viction. "I thought that I admired her
because I thought I ought to do it, that was
all. But I never heard anything in my life
with such pleasure as I did her very decided 'no.' Now you know the truth, and
do you think you will be able to forget
that I have been utterly scorned and set
aside, and say 'yes,' yourself?"

"But how do I know that you are not
mistaken now—that you are sure you care
anything for me, the girl of whom you did
not approve?"

"Look at me," he said, "and see."

Again she raised her eyes, met his glance
for an instant, and again looked quickly at
the floor.

"Dinah," he said, entreatingly, "say
'yes'!"

"Yes," she murmured, faintly but distinctly.

He reached forward as if to take her in
his arms, then, remembering where he was,
he straightened himself impatiently.

"Remember, Dinah," he said, "I am only a poor man. But I will try that you shall have what you want."

"Oh, I shall," she answered, gayly. "You know I am thought a very mercenary person, and I shall have everything."

"But how?" he demanded.

"In the surest way," she replied, looking at him with unaverted eyes; "not by choosing the things, but by choosing the man who is to give them to me."

And sliding her hand along by her side so that no one saw what she did, she took his hand firmly in her grasp.

THE END

www.ingramcontent.com/pod-product-compliance
Lightning Source LLC
Chambersburg PA
CBHW020901020726
47497CB00005B/1510